MURKY SEAS

A Rowan Gray Mystery Book 2

LILY HARPER HART

HarperHart Publications

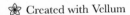

One

"That is nowhere near sexy enough."

Rowan Gray, her emerald green eyes focused on a simple summer dress with full sleeves and a below-the-knee hemline, had almost forgotten she wasn't shopping alone. Almost. The peace and the tranquility of the afternoon, the lazy breeze coming in from the water, made for a relaxing sensation that allowed Rowan's mind to aimlessly drift. Rowan's shopping pal, Sally Jenkins, simply wouldn't allow that to happen.

"What?" Rowan's cheeks colored as she shifted her eyes to the gregarious woman standing to her right. Sally Jenkins was a force of nature, her humidity-plagued hair piled in a messy bun at the back of her head as her eyes flashed with disdain when she gave the dress another look. Rowan was still getting used to the woman – she'd barely known her two weeks, after all – and she felt as if she was working overtime to keep up with her newfound friend's Bohemian charm.

"That dress isn't anywhere near sexy enough," Sally repeated, locking gazes with Rowan and arching a challenging eyebrow, as if daring her to put up a fuss when they were in public. "This is your first official date with Quinn. You need to look ... ."

Rowan's green eyes flashed with impatience as Sally searched for the correct word. "Slutty?"

"I was going to say 'unforgettable,'" Sally corrected, wagging a finger. "You shouldn't make snap judgments."

Rowan had the grace to look abashed. "I'm sorry. I didn't mean to do that. I just ... I'm not sure I feel comfortable wearing something revealing on a first date."

Sally ran her tongue over her teeth as she regarded Rowan. She couldn't decide if the woman was naturally shy or purposely obtuse about the way she looked. The one thing Sally did know for sure was that she'd never met a boundary – whether erected intentionally or otherwise – that she didn't want to cross.

"Okay, I'll play." Sally stepped closer, ignoring the two women watching the interplay two rows over. They looked to be in their thirties ... and busybodies. Sally couldn't stand a busybody ... unless she was the one busying herself with information about everyone else's bodies, that is. She'd purposely picked this stretch of stores for shopping because she knew Rowan would be unlikely to select anything flashy for her upcoming date with Quinn Davenport, the erstwhile head of security for the Bounding Storm, the cruise ship Rowan and Sally worked on together. The stores offered a variety of color and simple dress choices, which was exactly what Rowan needed.

Rowan knit her eyebrows, confused. "You'll play what?"

"The game," Sally replied, not missing a beat. "I'll play the game."

"I'm not playing a game."

"You are."

"I'm not."

"You are."

Rowan didn't bother to hide her annoyance. "I'm not playing a game," she gritted out. "I simply don't believe putting my goodies on display so strangers can ogle them is the proper way to start a relationship."

Sally pressed her lips together to keep from laughing. Rowan wasn't exactly a prude, but she was hardly an extrovert either. That was unusual for a cruise ship. Most of the people who signed up for the long hours and poor pay had ulterior motives for doing so, including a love of adventure or desire to find a man or woman to distract themselves with. Rowan was the exact opposite.

"You haven't even seen what I picked out yet," Sally pointed out.

"Oh, well … ." Rowan hardly wanted to admit that she'd made a snap judgment regarding Sally's clothing taste based solely on what she'd seen the woman wearing on the ship since their introduction.

"I like bright colors," Sally offered, scratching her cheek as she looked Rowan up and down. "I also know what looks good on people. Despite all that, I have no intention of changing your style. Your style is fine."

Rowan widened her green eyes, surprised. "It is?"

Sally almost took pity on the woman. She looked so lost. Then she remembered why she was there in the first place and squared her shoulders. "Come here." She grabbed Rowan's arm and jerked her in front of a full-length mirror. "What do you see when you look in there?"

Rowan swallowed hard, discomfort washing over her. "I … what?"

"You heard me." Sally refused to back down. "What do you see when you look in the mirror?"

Rowan studied her simple cargo shorts and tank top in

3

the reflective surface, her long auburn hair pulled back in a ponytail as her makeup-free face stared back at her. "I see me."

"Yes, and I see we're being literal today," Sally deadpanned, shaking her head. "I need to know what you see when you look in the mirror."

"I'm not sure what you're asking," Rowan admitted. "I see me when I look in the mirror. Do you think I'm going to see someone else there or something?"

Sally shook her head, amused. "I actually want you to describe how you look. For example ... ." Sally gripped Rowan's narrow hips and squared them toward the mirror. "What do you see here?"

"Your hands on my butt."

Sally snorted, giving Rowan's rounded rear end a good squeeze rather than releasing her. "Now my hands are on your butt. I was talking about your hips, though."

"Oh." Rowan chewed her bottom lip. "I see normal hips. Am I supposed to see something else?"

Sally made an exasperated face. "You know, for a photographer, you have extremely narrow vision."

Rowan pursed her lips as she considered the statement. Sally wasn't the first person to say that to her. In fact, her father said the same thing when she refused to agree with him about one of her high school classmate's propensity for stealing things when no one was looking. That was years ago, though, before he disappeared on the eve of her eighteenth birthday and left her to fend for herself, before she lost her job as a newspaper photographer and joined the staff of the Bounding Storm to keep herself financially afloat.

"I still see me," Rowan admitted after a beat. "I'm not sure what else you expect me to see, because ... well ... it's me in the mirror."

"Oh, geez." Sally rolled her eyes so hard Rowan worried she might topple over. "I want you to see yourself when you look in the mirror. I'm not trying to change you. I'm just trying to make you ... brighter."

Rowan glanced back at the dress she picked out – and Sally summarily dismissed – and sighed. Sally was right. The dress was plain, to the extreme of being boring. She didn't want to risk being boring now that she was going on an actual date with the security guru of her dreams. Heck, Quinn Davenport was the security guru of everyone's dreams. No joke. Once the rest of the female staff – and a handful of male staffers, too – found out that Quinn and Rowan were involved, the Bounding Storm became a hotbed of gossip and Rowan was suddenly popular with people she'd never even met.

"I'm not suggesting that we go crazy," Sally clarified, leading Rowan toward a rack that contained simple floral dresses. "Look at these, for example. They're cute. They're short, falling mid-thigh, which means you won't be showing off anything unless you bend way far over. If you bend that far over it's going to be on purpose, so I doubt you'll care if he sees anything at that point."

Rowan's cheeks flushed with color. "I ... ."

"Shh." Sally pressed a finger to her lips to quiet Rowan. "This green right here is a fun color, not quite neon but still bright, and it sets off your eyes." Sally held the simple shift up to Rowan's chest. "It's beautiful. I think you should try it."

Rowan glanced at the dress and immediately started shaking her head. "I can't wear that!" She was scandalized. "My boobs will fall out of that. Are you crazy?"

Sally glanced down at the dress a second time and then burst out laughing, her chuckles catching Rowan off guard. "You don't wear this without anything under it."

"Yes, but I'm not interested in showing off my bra strap," Rowan argued. "I'm too old for that."

"Oh, you're such a complainer." Sally shook her head, dumbfounded. "You don't wear a bra under this."

Rowan shifted from mildly worried to panicked. "What? Are you kidding? I'll fall out in every direction. We've already been over that."

"Wow, you're so much work." Sally made a big show of muttering to herself as she walked to another rack, returning with a pretty white tank top. "See this? This has the bra built right in. It's sleek and pretty, and has a beautiful lace neckline right here. You wear this under the dress."

"Oh." Things clicked into place for Rowan and she felt a little silly for overreacting. "That is pretty ... and it matches the dress well." She held the two items together, chewing her lip as she regarded them. "I guess I kind of made myself look stupid, huh?"

Sally wanted to nod. She wanted to agree without hesitation ... and yet she couldn't. Her expression softened when she saw the way Rowan stared at the dress, a momentary rush of sympathy washing over her. "You're really nervous, aren't you?"

Rowan snapped her head up, her cheeks burning brightly. "I ... no. Of course not. Why would I be nervous?" The words spilled out of her mouth at a rapid-fire pace.

"Because this is a big deal," Sally replied, unruffled. "You and Quinn have been shooting love daggers at one another with your eyes for two weeks. You've slept in the same bed ... several times, mind you ... and yet nothing more than some vigorous eye lusting has happened."

"We wanted to do it the right way," Rowan protested, her fingers plucking at non-existent nubs on the dress fabric. "We were busy with the sweet sixteen cruise over the last week and we just … wanted to wait until we had some time off."

Sally snorted. "I'm not saying it's a bad thing. I'm merely saying you've had a week to build it up in your head because Quinn insisted that your first date would happen off the ship. When you're living in a fishbowl like we are, that adds pressure because everyone is staring."

"I really like him," Rowan admitted, her voice small.

"He really likes you, too."

"Do you think?"

Sally fought the urge to roll her eyes when she saw the earnest expression on Rowan's face. The woman had no idea about her appeal. Sure, Quinn turned every female head on the ship – and he did it without noticing or caring – as he strode down the deck. Rowan managed to turn a few heads of her own since joining the staff. She was even more oblivious than Quinn, though. She didn't notice anything other than her camera and him, and he didn't notice anything other than his security concerns and her. It was quite entertaining to watch them flounder around one another at times.

"I think he definitely likes you." Sally bobbed her head. "I think he's going to like you even more in this outfit. You should try it on."

Rowan stared at the green dress before taking it and Sally couldn't help but wonder if the nervous woman was going to come up with some sort of excuse to get out of buying the frock. Instead, Rowan took them both by surprise when she clasped the dress to her chest and wandered into the dressing room, shutting the wicker door before stripping.

Sally perused the dress rack for something she might like as Rowan nervously chattered on the other side of the thin door. Sally offered Rowan the appropriate answers as the woman changed, and when she heard the door open, she shifted her eyes to the opening and smiled.

Rowan was a vision of loveliness – other than the fuzzy hair, which was a result of Florida's rampant humidity. The Bounding Storm was in dock for a few days as they prepared for another cruise. Nothing could be done about the humidity. Rowan was absolutely beautiful in the dress, though.

"I definitely think that's it," Sally said, beaming as Rowan moved to the mirror. "That dress matches your eyes and fits your body perfectly."

"Do you think?" Rowan wasn't convinced, chewing her lip as she studied her reflection. She was so caught up she didn't notice two men move to the spot next to Sally so they could watch her, too.

"I definitely think you should get the dress."

Rowan jolted at the voice, swiveling quickly. She forced a smile when she saw the two men, both of whom looked to be in their late twenties. They were quite handsome and Sally couldn't help but give them both an appraising look out of the corner of her eye.

"I'm sorry. I didn't see you standing there." Rowan's cheeks were already red thanks to the heat. The hue only deepened when she realized the two men were staring at her. "Am I in your way?"

"Oh, you're not in anybody's way." The man who spoke had blond hair and blue eyes, strong shoulders tapering to a narrow waist, and his cheekbones looked to have been chiseled out of stone. His eyes were lit with mirth as they roamed Rowan's bare legs. "You look great."

"I told you." Sally winked before focusing on the men. "Are you guys locals?"

"What? No. Sorry. We're just passing through the area.

We wouldn't mind taking the two of you out for dinner and drinks tonight, though. In fact, we would really enjoy that." This time it was the darker of the two men who spoke. He was just as handsome as his friend, although his hair and eyes were brown. He also had something of an accent, although Sally couldn't quite place it.

"Oh, well, that's sweet." Rowan kept her face pleasant even as her mind drifted. "I have other plans, though."

"Oh, that's too bad." The blond man's expression slipped. "You could always cancel those plans."

"Not bloody likely," Sally said snickering. When she realized the two men were watching her with curious gazes, she collected herself. "Rowan's plans are set in stone. Trust me. She won't change her mind on that."

"Ah, well, that's too bad." The dark-haired man made a soft clucking sound in the back of his throat. "I feel strangely depressed."

Sally bit the inside of her cheek to keep from laughing. These guys were good. They'd turned flirting into an art form. They clearly weren't used to anyone turning them down. "Yes, well, I'm free." The words were out of Sally's mouth before she had a chance to consider whether it was wise to utter them.

Rowan widened her eyes to comical levels, as if to say "what do you think you're doing," but Sally ignored her friend's obvious signs of distress.

"I happen to know a great bar that's close to the beach," Sally offered, grinning. "Rowan has plans but I'm sure I can scrounge up another friend or two if you guys want to meet us there."

The blond man turned his full attention to Sally, Rowan seemingly forgotten. "That sounds like a marvelous offer. What bar?"

"And what time?" the dark-haired man pressed.

Sally's smile was serene as Rowan turned back to her reflection. Rowan tuned out the rest of the date negotiations, and when she risked a glance over her shoulder, she found Sally standing by herself.

"Are you sure that's a good idea?" Rowan asked, a slight wave of worry niggling the back of her brain. "You don't know those guys. They could be dangerous."

"That's why I invited them to the bar where everyone from the Bounding Storm hangs out," Sally explained. "I can hang out with them and not be worried they're serial killers ... or something worse."

Rowan cocked a dubious eyebrow. "There's something worse than serial killers?"

"Thieves."

"Oh." Rowan didn't believe thieves were worse than serial killers, but she understood what Sally was getting at. If the two men were grifters and thought Sally had money to steal, they wouldn't hesitate to ply her with liquor while also trying to pilfer her wallet. "I feel better knowing you're going to be hanging around with people from the ship now that you mentioned that. You guys can watch each other's backs in case those men are up to no good."

"I've been at this a long time," Sally said. "I know what I'm doing." She smoothed the back of the dress and smiled. "This is definitely the outfit for your big date. Quinn is going to go non-verbal when he sees you in it."

Rowan returned the smile, genuinely thankful she'd managed to make a true friend in such a short amount of time. She bobbed her head as a helpful clerk shuffled closer. "I'll take this one ... the tank top, too."

Two

"How do I look?"

Demarcus Johnson sat on the chair at the far side of Quinn's room and arched an eyebrow as his friend fussed in front of the mirror, amused. He'd watched the normally taciturn security chief change his shirt no less than five times over the past hour.

"You look like a dreamboat," Demarcus teased, amused.

The corners of Quinn's mouth tipped down as he shifted a dark look over his shoulder. "You don't have to be here," he reminded the chatty head bartender. "If you're bored, by all means, the door is that way." Quinn jerked his thumb for emphasis.

Demarcus didn't bother muffling his snort and he was almost certain he heard Quinn mutter something about "not needing any of this" before turning back to his reflection. Quinn hadn't been on the ship all that long himself before Rowan showed up on the scene, although he certainly wasn't a newcomer. Over that time he'd been friendly with other workers but refused to embrace lasting bonds. That's why Demarcus took it upon himself to force a friendship. He figured Quinn needed it, whether he realized it or not. Life at sea could be lonely if you shut yourself off to possibility.

"You wanted me here," Demarcus reminded him.

"I did not!" Quinn's eyes flashed with protest. "You invited yourself to watch me get dressed, and you brought martinis, for that matter. I didn't invite you to do anything."

Demarcus ignored Quinn's tone. "Martinis you haven't so much as sipped yet."

"I'm not in the mood to drink." Quinn ran a hand over his dark hair before smoothing the front of his shirt. "I'm fine."

"Uh-huh." Demarcus dubiously downed the remainder of his martini. "This is a watermelon martini, man. I made it especially for you. You're hurting my feelings by not drinking it."

Quinn scowled, his dark eyes filling with disgust. "Are you trying to make me kill you? If so, you're doing a good job. I really do want to wrap my hands around your neck and give it a good squeeze."

Demarcus shrugged, unbothered. "I'm trying to get you to relax, man. You're coiled like a snake. If you're not careful, you're going to strike ... like a snake. Like a mean snake." Demarcus got lost in his description before regrouping. "What was I saying?"

"That I'm a snake." Quinn's tone was dry. "Then you got distracted by the sound of your own voice. I'm pretty sure that's the alcohol's fault."

"You say that like it's a bad thing." Demarcus flashed a winning smile, the stark white of his teeth standing out against the rich brown tones of his skin. "Dude, seriously, you need to take it down a notch. That's why I brought the martinis."

Quinn stared at him a moment, his expression unreadable. "I think I'm nervous." It was hard to admit, but the second the words left his mouth he felt better. "Seriously, dude, I think I'm nervous. I don't even know how it happened."

"You met a certain photographer and fell head over heels the second she opened her mouth."

Quinn shot Demarcus a withering look. "I hardly fell head over heels. I find her interesting. That's all."

Demarcus knew it was more than that, but he didn't want to risk pushing Quinn when he clearly wasn't ready to admit anything of the sort. He worried he might cause the man to take a step back, inadvertently hurting Rowan in the process. Quinn would come back – Demarcus was certain about that – but he didn't want to derail the Quinn and Rowan train before it had a chance to gain steam.

"She's an interesting woman," Demarcus said, pouring the remaining contents from his martini shaker to a glass and holding it up. "You're nervous because you really like her and you want this date to go well. That's why I brought this."

Quinn eyed the pink drink with distaste. "I don't want to get drunk."

"It's one drink, man," Demarcus prodded. "It will settle your nerves. Do you want Rowan to think you're a spaz? You're risking exactly that if you don't take a chill pill."

Quinn rubbed his chin. "Is that what the drink is, a chill pill?"

Demarcus nodded. "It's not enough alcohol to make you drunk. You need to calm down, though. You're making me nervous and I'm not even the one who will be kissing you tonight."

Quinn balked. "Don't say things like that!"

"I could kiss you if you think it will make you feel better." Demarcus winked, causing the corners of Quinn's mouth to curl. "In fact, if you don't taste my masterpiece, I'm going to chase you around this room until you do kiss me."

"See, now I know you're trying to make me uncomfortable." Quinn strode forward and grabbed the martini glass. "I'm not drinking this because I'm afraid of you trying to kiss me, so don't spread that rumor."

Demarcus mustered a perfunctory nod. "I wouldn't dream of it."

Quinn glared at the pink liquid. "I'm drinking this because I might throw up otherwise and it's freaking me out." He downed the drink in two large gulps, slamming the glass on the table before resting his hand on his stomach. "Okay, now I might throw up for a different reason. That thing was straight sugar."

Demarcus leaned back in his chair, grinning. "It will settle in a second and you'll be glad for it. Trust me."

Surprisingly, Quinn found he did trust the extroverted bartender. He couldn't explain why, but there was something open and warm about Demarcus Johnson. He actually enjoyed spending time with the man. "I'll take your word for it."

Quinn turned back to the mirror and ran his hand over his short-cropped hair. It wasn't long enough to style, which given the humidity today, was a good thing. "I'm ready."

"You look nice," Demarcus said, nodding approvingly at the black shirt and cargo shorts. "Out of curiosity, where are you taking her?"

"The seafood restaurant down on the beach," Quinn replied. "She loves crab legs and they have the best in the area. I reserved a table on the deck so we could relax."

"That sounds like a plan."

"Yeah." Quinn scratched his cheek as he glanced at the clock on the wall. He still had fifteen minutes before he had to pick up Rowan. "Maybe I should try another shirt."

Demarcus chuckled. "Knock yourself out, man."

"THIS IS A BEAUTIFUL SPOT."

Rowan worked overtime to tamp down her nerves as Quinn pulled out her chair for her. She flashed a smile as she sat, thankful for the night breeze as it kissed her skin and cut down on the overpowering heat from earlier in the day.

"I thought you might like it." Quinn returned the smile, hating the way his heart thumped in his chest as he struggled to relax. There was a reason he didn't date. He didn't like it. He didn't like getting to know someone. Heck, he didn't want to know anyone. That's what he always told himself, anyway. Of course, that changed when he met Rowan. He didn't feel as if he could discover enough of her secrets ... ever. The internal admission only made him feel more uneasy.

Rowan flipped open her menu and scanned it, her stomach rolling when she saw the prices. "We're both paying for our own meals, right?"

Quinn cocked an eyebrow, surprised. It was only then that he realized she was just as nervous as he was. "No." He shook his head. "This is a date. I'm buying dinner."

"But ... it's too expensive."

Quinn chuckled, the warm emotion attached to the sound allowing him the chance to unclench his fingers, which were busy holding the arms of the chair so tightly that his knuckles turned white. "I make more money than you," he reminded her. "Besides, it's a date. I'm not known for spending a lot of money so I have quite a bit put away. Don't worry yourself about it."

Rowan nodded, although she wasn't convinced. "Maybe I'll just get a salad."

Quinn scowled, not bothering to wipe the expression from his face when the waitress approached.

"Are you ready to order?"

Quinn nodded, never moving his gaze from Rowan's pretty features. "We'll have a bottle of the house merlot. We also want two orders of the Thunder Bay Feast."

Rowan scoured the menu for the item in question, her mouth dropping open when she realized what Quinn had ordered. "You can't be serious."

"Oh, I'm serious." Quinn leaned forward and snagged the menu from her hand. "I've seen you eat. I happen to know you like everything in that entrée and they have big portions here, which is good for both of us."

"That's a wonderful choice," the waitress said, adopting a flirty smile as she swayed back and forth in front of Quinn. "Do you want soup or salad?"

Quinn barely mustered a glance for the waitress, much to her chagrin, and instead remained focused on Rowan. "You can order that part yourself, right?"

Rowan's eyes darkened, but she flashed a grimace that resembled a smile and nodded. "I'll have the salad with ranch dressing."

"I'll have the same," Quinn said. "We need water to go with the wine, too."

"I'm on it."

Rowan waited for the waitress to disappear to make her feelings known. "It's too much. I have money back in my room. I'm going to pay you for my half of the bill when we get back."

"No, you're not." Quinn crossed his arms over his chest, squinting one eye as he regarded her. Strangely enough, the mere act of arguing with his date was enough to allow the unease to seep from his bones. "This is a date, Rowan. That means I pay."

"Only if you believe in antiquated sexual roles," Rowan shot back, unruffled. "I don't happen to believe in those roles, by the way. I believe a woman can do anything that a man can do … sometimes she can even do more."

Quinn's lips curved as he grabbed a breadstick from the basket at the middle of the table. "Oh, yeah? Can you bench press two hundred and fifty pounds?"

Rowan shrugged. "I have no idea. If I worked up to it, I'm guessing I could."

"Can you pee standing up?" Quinn smirked as he asked the question.

"Yes. It won't be hygienic, but yes. Can you have a baby?"

Quinn opened his mouth to answer and then snapped it shut. "Hmm."

"Didn't think of that, did you?"

"I guess I didn't." Quinn grinned as he leaned forward, handing half of the breadstick to Rowan. "This is going to be fun."

Rowan widened her eyes, surprised. "It is? Wait a second … you're getting off on the fighting."

"This is hardly what I would consider fighting," Quinn corrected. "I am enjoying the conversation, though. In truth, I was a bit nervous earlier. I have no idea why. The fact that you decided to pick a ridiculous fight eradicated all of my nervousness, though, so thank you."

"It was not a ridiculous fight."

"Oh, it was ridiculous."

Rowan rolled her neck, exasperation wafting off of her. "You're kind of a pain in the butt. Has anyone ever told you that?"

"More people than I can count on both hands."

"Well, you might want to take it to heart." Rowan took a bite of the breadstick and sighed, munching it thoroughly before continuing. "I was nervous, too. It seems ridiculous because we've spent so much time together over the past two weeks, but ... there it is."

Quinn's grin had a magical effect on Rowan's frayed nerves. "Well, you look beautiful. As for the nerves, something tells me we'll get over them."

"Oh, yeah? How?"

Quinn held his hands palms up. "Let's find out, shall we?"

Rowan realized what he was suggesting after a moment's contemplation. They'd been getting to know one another for two weeks. This was merely a continuation of that. There was no reason to be nervous. "Yeah. Let's find out."

TWO HOURS later Rowan stood in the shadow of the Bounding Storm, her sandals resting on a rock as she waded in the water and let the sand bunch between her toes. Her stomach hurt from laughing – Quinn was funnier than she gave him credit for – and she couldn't remember ever being this relaxed on a first date.

"It's your turn," she challenged, shifting toward him as he sat on the beach flipping through seashells. "What's your favorite horror movie?"

They'd asked each other a series of inconsequential questions over dinner before taking their game to a private spot on the beach. Quinn was thrilled with the meal, but the company was even better. They hadn't done anything big and yet he knew he would never forget this night.

"*Jaws.*"

Rowan stilled. "Are you serious?"

Quinn nodded. "I love that movie. It's a classic for a reason."

"But … you work on a cruise ship," she reminded him. "Don't sharks frighten you?"

"I don't really give them much thought. Do they frighten you?"

Rowan nodded without hesitation. "I dream about sharks a lot … weird dreams, where they come up from beneath the carpet and try to eat me in my bedroom and stuff."

"Really?" Quinn's eyebrows flew up his forehead. "I'm betting a psychiatrist would have a field day with that admission. What do you think it means?"

"That I don't want to get eaten alive."

Quinn chuckled, delighted. "You have a very literal mind sometimes."

"I know."

Quinn lifted a shell so he could study it in the muted moonlight and then added it to a pile on his right. "What's your favorite horror movie?"

"*The Shining.*"

Now it was Quinn's turn to be surprised. "That's a little darker than I was expecting."

"Oh, yeah? What were you expecting?"

"I thought you were going to say something like *Shaun of the Dead* or *Zombieland.* You know, mix a bit of humor with your horror. I didn't realize you liked serious horror movies."

"I do like horror movies." Rowan pursed her lips as she

hopped from one foot to the other, enjoying the way the water rushed around her calves. "My father was a horror movie fanatic and we used to watch movies together on the weekends quite often."

"Ah." Quinn knew that Rowan's father disappeared almost ten years before, leaving an orphaned girl on the cusp of adulthood to fend for herself. He had no idea what happened to the man – only that Rowan spoke fondly of him – but he was angry on her behalf. He wasn't angry because the man was gone. Rowan believed he was dead and Quinn couldn't help but agree. They simply hadn't found his body yet. He was angry that she was left alone at such an impressionable age. She didn't know it, but she was marked by the experience. It made her standoffish – apparently with everyone but him. "What about science fiction? Do you like science fiction?"

"Like space movies?" Rowan wrinkled her nose. "Are you a Trekkie?"

Quinn grinned, legitimately amused. "I like *Star Trek*. I wouldn't call myself a Trekkie, though."

"What would you call yourself?"

"Easily entertained." Quinn dusted off his hands as he stood, taking Rowan by surprise when he offered her a seashell. "This is for you ... to remember our first date."

Rowan watched as Quinn dropped the shell into the palm of her hand, smiling when she saw the delicate purple accents. "It's beautiful."

"So are you."

Quinn's response was simple and it caused Rowan to suck in a breath when she lifted her chin and found Quinn staring at her. They were close, their faces only inches apart. All Quinn had to do was lean in closer and press his lips against hers and then ... .

"What are you thinking?" Rowan felt breathless.

"That this has been a great night."

"It has." Rowan bobbed her head. "The shell is beautiful, but I didn't need it to remember this night. I'm pretty sure I won't be able to forget."

"I was thinking the same thing."

"Really?"

Quinn nodded as he leaned a tad closer. "In fact ... ." Whatever he was about to say died on his lips when the sound of sirens assailed his ears. He jerked his head up, years of military training taking over as he took a protective stance in front of Rowan.

"They're not coming for us," Rowan said, resting her hand on his forearm. "They're going down there." Rowan pointed to a spot down the beach. It had to be a good half mile away, but since it was a clear night, no clouds in sight, the myriad of police lights were obvious in the darkness. "I wonder what they're doing."

"I don't know." Quinn absentmindedly rubbed Rowan's back as he pressed her body closer to his. "Let's go back to the ship, though. It's getting late."

Rowan acquiesced without complaint. "By the way, thank you for dinner."

Quinn pursed his lips as he dragged his attention away from the swirling lights and focused on his date. "Thank you for the new dress ... and the conversation ... and your smile."

Rowan was thankful that it was dark because she could feel her cheeks burning. "How did you know it was a new dress?"

"It was just a hunch."

"Okay, well ... shall we go?" Rowan held out her hand. She almost looked timid as she waited for Quinn to take it.

"Let's go." Quinn's hand was warm when it wrapped

around hers. "So, you're not a Trekkie, huh? How do you feel about *Star Wars*?"

"I like the ewoks."

Quinn heaved out a long-suffering sigh. "Oh, woman, we need to talk."

Three

"How was your date?"

Demarcus peeled himself away from the wall outside of Quinn's room the following morning, causing the security chief to take an inadvertent step back as he struggled to control his confusion. He was still waking up and he needed a jolt of caffeine to jumpstart his weary mind.

"Have you been waiting out here all night?"

Demarcus snorted. "No. I decided to swing by before hitting breakfast." He cast a sidelong look at Quinn's closed door. "I'm taking it there was no action besides kissing, huh? That's okay. You'll get there."

Quinn made a disgusted face. "Not that I'm not happy to see you but ... ."

"Of course you're happy to see me." Demarcus waved off whatever Quinn was about to say with haphazard nonchalance. "Everyone is always happy to see me."

"Yes, well, aside from that ... ."

"How did Rowan look last night?" Demarcus blathered on. "Sally said she bought a dress and was nervous about wearing it in front of you. I'll bet she looked adorable."

"She looked beautiful but ... ."

"I know you were probably hoping to get some action, but you've got time," Demarcus offered. "Unless ... you didn't have sex with the girl and then leave to sleep in your own bed, did you? That's extremely tacky."

Quinn's expression shifted from mildly annoyed to completely enraged. "I didn't do that!"

Demarcus heaved out a sigh, relieved. "Good. That would've been hard to recover from. I know you don't have a lot of experience with women ... er, scratch that ... I know that you don't have a lot of experience having a long-term relationship with women, but that is a serious no-no."

Quinn stopped walking, gripping his hands together as he glared at Demarcus' back. By the time the other man shifted to meet his gaze, the bartender's mischievous grin was obvious.

"You were joking," Quinn said after a beat.

Demarcus bobbed his head. "I was. You need to learn to absorb a joke and laugh at yourself, man."

"I don't find having sex with a woman and leaving her alone in the middle of the night particularly funny."

"Neither do I. That's why making a joke about it becomes funny. Don't you get it?"

Quinn shook his head. "Not even remotely."

"You will eventually." Demarcus clapped Quinn's back as the man fell into step with him. "Seriously, though, how was your date? You don't seem very excited."

"I was excited until I saw you," Quinn countered, scratching his cheek. "The date was good, though. We were both nervous at the start, but we settled in pretty quickly."

"Did she like the restaurant?"

Quinn smiled at the memory of Rowan inhaling her crab legs. "She liked the restaurant."

"Good. What did you do after?"

"Honestly? We took a walk on the beach and talked. We were out there until almost midnight. The only reason we came back when we did is because the cops showed up on the beach about a half mile down and it kind of ruined the ambiance."

"Oh, I heard about that." Demarcus appeared thoughtful as he tapped his chin. "It was on the news when I was shaving this morning."

Quinn managed to drag his mind away from the way Rowan looked when he dropped her off at her room – and chickened out before giving her a goodnight kiss – and fully focused on Demarcus for the first time since he found the man standing outside of his room. "What did they say?"

"They found a body," Demarcus replied, missing the change in Quinn's demeanor. "It was a young woman – I think she was only twenty-five or so, if I remember right – and some night fishermen hooked her body instead of a marlin or something."

"Really?" Quinn arched an eyebrow. "That was lucky."

"I don't think the fishermen feel the same way. Maybe they weren't fishing for marlin. Do they have trout in saltwater?"

"Not that." Quinn flicked Demarcus' ear, shaking his head as he ignored the question. "I mean that they found her. She could've been swept out to sea and no one would've been the wiser. At least this way her family will be able to put her to rest."

"There is that," Demarcus acquiesced. "I was just joking about the fishermen being upset. That's probably the most action they've seen in weeks."

"That's an even worse joke," Quinn pointed out. "What did the news report say? How was the woman killed?"

"Oh, um, I can't really remember." Demarcus darted his eyes to the docking area as they hit the main deck. "I think the cops were still waiting for confirmation from the medical examiner but they believed it was an accidental death ... something about finding a bottle of vodka on the beach next to the woman's shoes."

"Oh." Quinn turned his military mind inwards. "She probably got drunk and decided to go for a little swim, maybe got caught in the current or something. She's lucky she didn't run into a predator out there. Sharks stick relatively close to the shoreline in this area."

"Uh-huh." Demarcus was clearly distracted, but Quinn didn't bother to figure out why.

"By the way, did you know Rowan is afraid of sharks? She mentioned it last night when we were talking about horror movies. I said my favorite horror movie was *Jaws* and she thought that was weird."

Demarcus finally dragged his incredulous eyes from the dock and focused on his friend. "You talked about horror movies on your first date? May I ask why?"

"We talked about everything on our date," Quinn corrected. "As for why ... I guess because we could. Once we started talking, we didn't stop."

Demarcus' lips quirked. "It sounds like you had a magical time."

"We did." Quinn kept the part about being too afraid to kiss Rowan goodnight to himself. Even though he'd let fear get the better of him, he was fairly certain he would get a chance to rectify the situation. "It was a great night."

"Oh, you're so cute, you smitten kitten." Demarcus grabbed Quinn's cheek and gave it a good jiggle before inclining his chin toward the dock. "As much as I don't want to be the rain cloud on your sunny day, I forgot what we were dealing with on this cruise until just now. We need to get a few things in order as soon as we're done with breakfast."

"Why?" Quinn racked his brain. He'd seen the briefing from the captain the previous day. After a cursory look – and nothing to tip him off that they would be dealing with anything even remotely resembling an unruly crowd – Quinn discarded the briefing on his desk so he could focus on the date.

"Take a look." Demarcus' smile was tight and grim.

Quinn swiveled his head, widening his eyes when he saw the bevy of women flocking toward the dock. That was all he could see, for as far as his gaze would travel. Women. Big women. Small women. Blond women. Brunette women. So very many women. They were hurrying toward the dock so they could board the ship. The only thing they all had in common were pink blazers and matching briefcases. "What the ... ."

"Cara G Cosmetics," Demarcus supplied. "It's their annual convention. I had no idea they were arriving today. I must've blocked it out."

Quinn furrowed his brow. "Cara G. Cosmetics? That's like Mary Kay, right?"

"Mary Kay isn't like Mary Kay used to be. It's the same general principle, though. The sales representatives earn things like cars and jewelry for being top sellers. It's a pretty cutthroat business."

Quinn inadvertently snorted despite Demarcus' serious expression. "They're women selling mascara and stuff. You make them sound like open water pirates."

"Just wait."

"Seriously?" Quinn couldn't stop himself from laughing. "You're scared of a bunch of makeup hawking women?"

"Just wait."

"Oh, whatever." Quinn guffawed loudly as he slapped Demarcus' back. "Look at them. They're wearing pink blazers, for crying out loud. Exactly how bad could they be?"

"Just wait."

WELL, THIS is very ... not what I ordered."

Rowan kept her smile in place, her camera gripped in her hands, and met Daphne DuBois' harsh gaze with an even one of her own.

"I'm not sure what you mean." Rowan shifted her eyes to the specialty backdrop that had been designed specifically for Cara G Cosmetics representatives. She'd only been responsible for taking photographs at two arrivals so far, but as far as she could tell the gaudy pink backdrop seemed par for the course. "You ordered something else?"

Daphne nodded, her perfect blond hair moving like a helmet as she did. "It's the wrong pink."

Rowan widened her eyes, confused. "I ... don't understand."

"This is salmon pink," Daphne supplied. "I specifically ordered baby pink."

"There's a difference?" Rowan didn't consider herself an expert on the color pink, but she couldn't figure out why Daphne was complaining.

"Of course there's a difference." Daphne made a tsking sound as she lifted her briefcase and held it against the cardboard floral monstrosity. Rowan had been horrified when first laying eyes on it, but after a few minutes of contemplation she merely shrugged and started taking photographs of incoming guests. She didn't feel it was her place to judge. Daphne clearly felt otherwise.

"See this," Daphne prodded. "My blazer is baby pink. This backdrop is salmon pink. They totally clash."

"Well ... ." Rowan licked her lips. She saw no difference in the shades of pink. In fact, if it weren't for Daphne's hair, she was convinced the woman could be swallowed by the cardboard pink cutout and never be seen or heard from again. "They look like the same pink to me."

"Then you're clearly blind," Daphne snapped. "This won't do at all."

"Well, this was what your company provided." Rowan chose her words carefully. "The cruise liner didn't pick out this backdrop. Cara G Cosmetics delivered this backdrop. I know. I asked."

"I understand that." Daphne tugged on her blazer to keep it from bunching at her narrow waist. "I am the president of Cara G Cosmetics. This is simply not the color I signed off on when I told them to manufacture the backdrop."

"Oh, well ... I don't know what to tell you."

"Of course you don't." Daphne took Rowan by surprise when she patted her arm in a dismissive way. "You're a minimum wage employee. You're only doing the best you can. I understand that. I'll take up the matter with my employees. Who knows, perhaps someone will become a former employee."

Rowan bit the inside of her cheek to refrain from saying something snarky. "That's probably the best way to handle things. Do you want your photograph taken in front of it or not?"

"Oh, well ... I guess I have no choice." Daphne flounced to a spot in front of the flowers, rested her briefcase on the floor, planted her hands on her hips, and struck a pose straight out of a Macy's catalog. "I photograph best from the left side. Make sure you get that profile."

"I'm on it." Rowan snapped a series of photographs in quick succession, making sure to look over the images on the back of the camera before sending Daphne on her way. She had a feeling if she didn't come out with something Daphne deemed "decent" she would have to do everything a second time, and she didn't want to spend one more minute with the woman than she had to.

Rowan frowned when she pulled up the first photo, her heart skipping when she caught sight of the familiar symbol hanging in space over Daphne's shoulder. She mechanically flipped through the other photos, but it was present in each one.

"Is that it?" Daphne asked, her patience wearing thin.

"Um … ."

"Let me see." Daphne jostled Rowan's arm and took the camera, seemingly oblivious of the symbol as she scanned the photographs. "That one." She nodded her head to make sure Rowan understood which photo she preferred. "Don't make the mistake of picking one of the other photos. I don't like them and I would hate to see you lose your job over picking the wrong photo."

Rowan's mouth was dry, but she nodded. "Yes, I would hate that, too." She watched Daphne move off in the direction of a small group of women, her heart thudding as she reached for her phone. Daphne Dubois was an unpleasant woman, but Rowan could hardly ignore what she saw in the camera.

"I'll be right with you," she called absentmindedly to the next woman in line. "I just have to do something first."

. . .

"THESE **WOMEN** ARE ANIMALS," Quinn complained for what felt like the fiftieth time in the last hour. He'd managed to extricate himself from another clingy woman with a cocktail in her hand as she tried to run her hands up and down his chest. "They're all in heat or something."

Demarcus, positioned behind the deck bar, snorted as he mixed a fruity drink. "I told you."

"You didn't tell me this," Quinn countered. "You kept saying 'just wait' and then laughing like a loon. You didn't tell me I was waiting for this, and if you had, I would've opted to hide in my room for the entire cruise."

"And miss out on all this fun? I'm shocked you would even consider that." Demarcus flashed a flirty wink as an energetic woman in pink leggings scampered up to the bar. "What would you like, sugar?"

"I want sex on the beach."

"Oh, honey, we all want that."

The woman giggled. "I want the drink Sex on the Beach," she corrected, her eyes sliding to Quinn, giggling when she realized exactly how much she liked what she saw. "I wouldn't mind the other type of sex on the beach with him, though."

"You need to get in line," Demarcus teased, clearly enjoying Quinn's discomfort. "I think our security chief is going to be very popular this cruise."

"Security chief?" The woman's eyes flashed. "That makes him even hotter. Honey, I don't suppose you have handcuffs, do you? If so, you can arrest me anytime."

Quinn forced a smile even as his stomach rolled. "Yes, well ... I think I'll manage to refrain from arresting you."

"Not for long because I plan on being very naughty." The woman took her drink from Demarcus and grinned. "I just love these yearly conventions."

Quinn watched her scurry off, letting his forced smile

drop once he was sure she was done looking back in his direction. "This is terrible. How are we supposed to put up with this for days?"

"If it's any consolation, they tip really well."

"I don't make my living off tips."

"Well, then you have absolutely nothing to look forward to." Demarcus didn't bother hiding his impish grin. "That sucks for you, huh?"

"You're on my last nerve," Quinn muttered, digging in his pocket when he heard his phone ring. His demeanor brightened considerably when he recognized Rowan's name on the screen. "Speaking of looking forward to things ... ." He slid his thumb over the screen and pressed the phone to his ear. "Good morning, sunshine. Do you miss me already?"

Demarcus snorted at Quinn's flirty tone. "You're such a smooth talker. You're going to break hundreds of hearts if you're not careful, stud."

Quinn ignored him. "What's up?"

Rowan was timid on the other end of the phone. "I hate to bother you but ... um ... I need you."

Quinn sobered immediately. "What's going on?"

"I saw it again." Rowan didn't have to explain what she saw in the photographs. Quinn knew about her special ability, about the death omen that haunted her every move. He not only knew the truth, but he believed her, which made him almost perfect in Rowan's eyes.

"You saw something in your camera?" Quinn lowered his voice and took a step away from Demarcus in an attempt to keep the conversation private. "Is it the thing we talked about?"

"Yes."

"Where are you?"

"I'm in the main lobby taking photographs of the new

guests," Rowan replied. "I think I'm going to need your help."

"I'm on my way. Hold tight."

"Thank you."

"There's no need to thank me," Quinn corrected. "We're in this together. I'll be there just as soon as I can. It's going to be okay."

Rowan could only hope that was true. If history was any indication, things were about to get a whole lot worse before they got better.

Four

Rowan kept snapping photographs even though she was agitated while waiting for Quinn. There were five hundred Cara G Cosmetics sales representatives due to hit the ship before leaving port and they made up the bulk of the guests this go around. Rowan had her work cut out for her, but thankfully almost everyone else either ignored or didn't notice the offending shade of pink on the backdrop.

Quinn found his way to the main lobby fairly quickly, his strong body and rugged good looks earning catcalls from the women waiting in line. He did his best to ignore the attention as he headed toward Rowan, but his cheeks were burning when he stopped in front of her.

Despite the serious situation, Rowan couldn't help but smile. "I see you're popular with our new guests."

"Yes, they love me." Quinn's face was impassive. "They keep asking me if I want to help them rouge their cleavage, whatever that means. One asked me if I wanted to have sex on the beach while ordering a drink."

Rowan pursed her lips. "Ah, it must be difficult to be a

sex symbol. You're like every woman's teenage dream. You should be on the cover of Teen Beat or something."

Quinn refused to crack a smile. "Did you need something, Ms. Gray."

Rowan stilled, put off by his chilly attitude. "I'm sorry. I didn't mean to offend you. I was just teasing."

Quinn's expression softened instantly. "No, I'm sorry. That wasn't fair. It's just ... ." He leaned closer so he could whisper, involuntarily shuddering when he got a whiff of her body spray. "They're animals. You know that, right? They keep threatening to eat me alive."

Rowan snorted as she patted his arm, letting her fingers linger for a few extra seconds. She had no idea why she was so captivated by him today. They'd spent the entire previous evening talking and getting to know one another and yet she almost felt as if she was going through withdrawal.

"Oh, um what was I saying?" Rowan jerked her hand back when she realized he was staring at her with an odd expression on his face.

"You were teasing me about my heartthrob status," Quinn reminded her. "It almost made me cry and you were debating about how you should make it up to me later when we're alone."

Rowan swished her lips. "I'm fairly certain that second part was never mentioned."

"That doesn't mean you weren't thinking it." Quinn lightly tapped her forehead and then sobered. "You called me, remember? What did you see?"

"Oh, right." Rowan grabbed Quinn's arm and dragged him away from the ogling women, lowering her voice as she locked gazes with him. "There's a woman. Her name is Daphne DuBois." She clicked through her photographs until she found the right one. "She's the president of Cara G Cosmetics."

"Okay." Quinn rubbed the back of his neck. "I see your symbol managed to make it in the backdrop here." Quinn leaned back and studied the physical backdrop a few feet away with unflinching eyes. "And it's not in the backdrop when I look at it now."

"No." Rowan bobbed her head. "I told you what that means for her."

"You did."

"Um ... ." Rowan broke off and chewed on her bottom lip, unsure how to proceed. When Quinn first asked her out, admitting he wanted to try a relationship even though he'd previously been against it, she worried they would spend their entire first date talking about her ability. She'd been forced to tell him about it two weeks before when another guest went missing. Instead of reacting with suspicion and disbelief, he believed her. Still, it was human nature to be curious. She thought his nature would force him to ask an endless stream of questions she couldn't answer because ... well ... she had no idea why she could see the death omen through her camera. She simply could. She expected Quinn to exhaust himself asking questions and grow frustrated when she provided no real answers. In reality it didn't even come up, which she hadn't bothered to notice until right now.

"What's wrong?" Quinn instinctively reached up and slipped a strand of her flyaway hair behind her ear. He could sense her discomfort and wanted to eradicate it. Sadly, he had no idea how to do that. Soothing someone is one of those things people learn to do over time. He wasn't there yet.

Rowan opted to be blunt. "Do you still believe me? I mean ... if you don't ... I understand. I just ... ."

"Shh." Quinn pressed his finger to her lips to silence her. "I believe you. Don't work yourself up into knots."

Rowan's mouth dropped open. "Did you just shush me?"

Quinn's frown flipped in the other direction. "Perhaps. I'm sorry. I just didn't want you beating yourself up. I believe you. Don't worry yourself about that. I'm simply trying to figure out what to do."

"Oh." Rowan was momentarily placated. "Well, I'm sorry."

"You don't need to be sorry, Trixie," Quinn teased, referring to Rowan's favorite teenage private detective, Trixie Belden. He'd turned the knowledge into something of a nickname, which Rowan secretly enjoyed because he always uttered the endearment with a smile. "So this woman's name is Daphne DuBois?"

Rowan nodded.

"I don't suppose you know where she's staying, do you?"

"I looked it up while you were heading in this direction," Rowan replied. "She's on the fifth floor, suite 512. The thing is, she said she was heading to the deck to drink with a group of her top sellers when she was leaving. I kind of eavesdropped on her."

"I don't blame you. Let me see the photo again."

Rowan acquiesced and Quinn stared at it for a long moment.

"Okay, all of these women look the same to me," Quinn admitted after a beat. "Can you send a copy of that to my phone?"

"Yes."

"Great. I will watch her until you're done here. Then I need you to meet me on the deck so we can come up with a plan of action. Does that work for you?"

Rowan heaved out a sigh as she bobbed her head. "Yes. Thank you so much."

"You don't need to thank me." Quinn shifted from one foot to the other, her earnest expression tugging on his heartstrings. He was dying to kiss her, offer her something to ease the strain playing at the corners of her eyes. There was no way he would let their first official kiss happen in front of an audience, though – especially an audience that wouldn't stop staring at him as if he was the last shrimp next to the cocktail sauce. On the flip side, Quinn couldn't force himself to walk away after doing nothing so he acted impulsively, grabbing the sides of her face and pressed a kiss to her forehead. "I'll meet you on the deck as soon as you're done here."

Quinn didn't bother to monitor Rowan's expression even though he was curious. Instead he turned on his heel and walked out of the room. Rowan momentarily fanned herself despite the fact that she was indoors and covered by air conditioning as she watched him flee. When she turned to the backdrop she found a brunette eyeing her quizzically.

"I'm so sorry," Rowan forced out. "I had to talk to the chief of security, but I can finish up now."

The woman waved off Rowan's apology. "Honey, if I had a man who looked like that, I'd spend my days coming up with security emergencies and ignoring the camera altogether. Don't worry about it."

"I HAVE A PROBLEM."

Rowan didn't bother with pleasantries when she found Quinn on the deck a few hours later, instead grabbing his iced tea and sucking down half of it before heaving herself in the chair and fixing him with a pointed look.

"The fish flies at midnight."

Rowan stilled, confused. Quinn's face was placid, but she couldn't figure out why he uttered those particular words. "Are you feeling hot? I mean ... do you have heat stroke?"

Quinn snorted, amused. "It's a joke, Rowan. I guess I'm not the only one who doesn't get the joke sometimes."

"The fish flies at midnight." Rowan mulled over the words. "I don't get it."

"It's simply that you walked up and announced you had a problem and it didn't seem to fit the conversation I was expecting," Quinn explained. "It sounded like code. It doesn't matter, though, I'm over the joke. What's your problem?"

"Look at this." Rowan slapped the camera in Quinn's hands and shifted her chair so she could move closer to him. "That's Penny Parker."

"Penny Parker?" Quinn arched an amused eyebrow. "That's like the most unfortunate name ever."

"I think it's kind of cute," Rowan hedged. "She's cute, too. She's sweet and has a really high voice. She also has really big boobs and a tiny little waist. I was a little jealous when I took her photograph."

Quinn's eyebrows inched up his forehead. "You have no reason to be jealous of anyone. Trust me."

Rowan's cheeks flushed with color. "Oh, well, thank you."

"Oh, geez." Quinn ran his hand over the back of his head. "You're uncomfortable with a compliment. If I have one complaint about you, it's that."

Rowan held her hands palms up and shrugged. "I'll work on it."

"Good."

"Just as soon as you work on accepting your position as ship heartthrob," she added, causing Quinn to scowl.

"Oh, that wasn't even remotely cute." Quinn made a growling sound as he focused on the photograph. "Okay, this is Penny Parker. I see what you were saying about the boobs."

Now it was Rowan's turn to scowl. "Don't be a pig."

"Oink, oink." Quinn sobered as he stared at the photo. "She has the omen behind her head, too."

"Exactly." Rowan exhaled heavily to steady herself. "She was the third-to-last person to come through the line. I talked to her a little bit after she was done because I wanted to keep her around until I finished. It didn't quite work out that way, but I did ask her some questions."

"Okay. What did you find out?"

"She's Daphne DuBois' assistant."

Quinn stilled, surprised. "Well, that's convenient." He peered closer at the photograph. "Does that mean something bad is going to happen to Daphne and Penny at the same time?"

"That's what I thought." Rowan snatched back the camera. "I think you've had plenty of time with Penny's boobs."

"I agree." Quinn's grin was sly. "I haven't had nearly enough time with yours, though."

Rowan blushed furiously as she thumbed through the photographs. "I can't believe you said that. I think my face is on fire."

"I know. That's why I said it." Quinn was relatively proud of himself. "That doesn't mean I didn't mean it."

"I ... cannot talk about this right now."

"Duly noted."

"I might not ever be able to talk about it," Rowan added.

"You'll get over that." Quinn thrummed his fingers on the table, content to watch Rowan study her camera until she shoved it back in front of his face.

"What do you make of that?" Rowan challenged.

"What?" Quinn stared at the photo for a long time. "Why am I back to looking at Daphne DuBois?"

"Because the omen is gone."

Quinn leaned forward, intrigued, all thought of flirting flying out to sea. "But ... how?"

"That's a very good question," Rowan replied. "I have no idea how it happened, or why it happened, or if it's going to stay that way. All I know is that Daphne now appears to be in the clear and Penny is the one in danger."

"Has this happened before?"

"I ... guess." Rowan said the words, but she didn't look certain. "I've managed to change a few things in certain cases and save people. I've never seen the omen hop from one person to another by itself, though. Whatever changed happened on this ship, and I have no idea why."

"I don't think the why is necessarily important," Quinn hedged. "All we know right now is that we need to watch Penny Parker."

"Yes, and keep an eye on Daphne DuBois in case something changes and the omen returns."

"I hadn't considered that." Quinn licked his lips. "My biggest problem is that all of these women look alike. They also dress alike and sound alike. I have no idea how I'm supposed to keep an eye on one of them when I can't tell them apart."

Rowan didn't bother to hide her surprise. "You think they all look alike?"

"Don't you?"

"I think that's a man thing to say. Do I look like all of them, too? If I were to hop in some pink leggings and

41

carry around one of those little briefcases, would you be able to pick me out of a crowd?"

Quinn's grin returned. He loved it when she got feisty. "Yes, but that's because I'm specifically attracted to you. I could pick you out of a thousand-person riot … or protest … or stampede. You're also different and look nothing like those women."

"Is that a good or bad thing?"

"It's definitely a good thing. I like the way you look."

"Even better than Penny Parker's boobs?"

Quinn smirked. "Surprisingly so. In fact … ." He didn't get a chance to finish because two of the Cara G Cosmetics women picked that moment to approach. He was fairly certain he recognized both of them, and the look on Harper's face told him she did, too. He absentmindedly flipped through the two photos she had bookmarked on the camera and kept his emotions in check when he realized he was looking at Daphne DuBois and Penny Parker. "Do you need something, ladies?"

Daphne shot Quinn an appreciative look as she scanned his well-muscled body. "I'm sure something can be arranged."

Quinn's smile was tight as he stared down at the woman. "I'm Quinn Davenport, chief of security. This is Rowan Gray. She's the ship's photographer. If you need help with something … ."

"Yes, yes." Daphne waved off Quinn's chilly reception. "I met Ms. Gray before and we've been looking for you. We were hoping to get a tour of the ship."

"Oh, well, I'm sure you can get a porter for that," Quinn said, shifting his eyes to the crowd. "I don't see one this very moment, but I'm sure one should be around."

"Yes, but … um … I want you to do it," Daphne prodded.

Quinn risked a glance at Rowan and found her staring at Penny. She didn't even bother glancing in his direction. "I'm not really a tour guide," Quinn hedged.

"No, but I'm very interested in the security business," Daphne prodded. "Very, very interested."

Quinn could read between the lines. What she was really saying was that she was very interested in him. "I can call a porter for you. Someone will be here within five minutes. You shouldn't have to wait long."

"That's not what I want." Daphne's voice was firm enough that it drew Rowan out of her reverie and she widened her eyes when she saw the cosmetic guru cross her arms over her chest.

"What's going on?" Rowan asked, confused.

"Ms. DuBois here is insisting I give her a tour," Quinn replied. "I explained that I would get a porter to do it, but she didn't seem all that interested."

"Oh, well … ." Rowan rolled her neck until it cracked, her mind busy. "Quinn would love to give you a tour," she announced after a beat.

Quinn swallowed his agitation as he leaned forward. "Excuse me?"

"You would love to give them a tour," Rowan repeated. "It will give you a chance to get to know some of the important Cara G Cosmetics faces. They're very important clients, after all."

Quinn stared at her a moment, things shifting into place. "Oh, right." He forced his gaze to Daphne and somehow mustered a smile. "I would love to give you a tour."

Daphne beamed as she fluffed her hair. "Great. I can't wait."

"That makes two of us."

Five

"There you are."

Quinn found Rowan sitting in a small alcove staring at her phone shortly before dinner. He'd spent the better part of the afternoon showing Daphne and her "executive team" around the ship. Listening to inane chatter for hours on end wasn't his favorite option when it came to work, but he shouldered the burden for as long as he could before walking Daphne back to her room and returning to his so he could shower. For some reason Daphne's rampant attention and veiled innuendo made him feel dirty.

"Hey. How was your tour?" Rowan didn't bother glancing up from her phone.

"Hellish. How was your afternoon?"

Rowan shrugged, noncommittal. "Busy. They set up a special online shopping window for those photos and I had to upload everything from this afternoon. I got an email reminding me to upload photos at least three times a day so Daphne can see that I'm doing my job, too. I'm really starting to dislike that woman."

Quinn arched an eyebrow as he sat across from her,

kicking his feet out in front of him as he sighed. "Don't you want to hear about my afternoon?"

"That's why I asked. You said it was hellish. I figured you would expound on that when you were ready."

Quinn worked hard to tamp down his agitation ... and failed. "Are you even paying attention to me?"

Rowan tore her gaze away from her phone. "I'm sorry. Did something happen?"

"Not particularly but ... what are you looking at?"

"The photos." Rowan was sheepish. "I wanted to see if the omen switched."

"Did it?"

"No. It's still on Penny."

"Well, that gives us someone to focus on." Quinn took the phone from her hand and flicked through the photos. "I tried to talk to Penny during the tour so I could get a feel for her as a person, maybe even figure out if she had plans to be in a specific part of the ship tonight, but it wasn't exactly easy."

"That was smart. Did you get anywhere?"

Quinn shook his head. "Daphne interrupted whenever I talked to anyone but her. She seemed determined to suck up all of the available oxygen."

"We're on a ship," Rowan pointed out, her pragmatic nature taking over. "Half of the ship is outside and has unlimited oxygen."

"That should give you some idea about how much she talks."

Rowan pressed her lips together to keep from laughing. "I'm sorry. You look miserable and that's on me. I thought it was a good opportunity."

"It *was* a good opportunity," Quinn conceded. "It was a good idea. That doesn't mean it wasn't painful."

"Oh, are you injured?" Rowan feigned sympathy. "Do you want me to kiss it and make it better?"

That's exactly what Quinn wanted, but he couldn't very well admit that in a busy hallway. Rowan realized what she said when it was too late to take it back, skillfully averting her eyes as her cheeks flushed with color. Quinn opted to let her off the hook rather than push things given their current location and the steady stream of foot traffic passing by.

"As far as I can tell, Daphne DuBois is a control freak," he offered, turning the conversation to something professional. "She thinks a lot about herself and she's interested in pretending to elevate the other women."

"Pretending?"

"That's what I said."

"So you're saying she doesn't really want to elevate the other women, simply caring that it appears as if that's her goal," Rowan prodded. "If she's only pretending, what's her real agenda?"

"I've been around enough women to know that she's really being passive aggressive and trying to break them down so she feels superior," Quinn replied. "She'll compliment one woman's shoes and then add something about how that poor woman probably has no choice but to buy from a discount store because she has such big feet."

Rowan widened her eyes, surprised. "Seriously? Did she do that in front of other people?"

"Just her little cronies. Why? Is that important."

Rowan held her hands palms up. "It's kind of a territorial thing. I saw it a lot when I was at the newspaper. The women were always in competition with one another that way. It was more the reporters than the photographers, though. I was the only female photographer and I got along fine with my co-workers."

"That's because you're cute." Quinn winked as he leaned back his head and stared at the ceiling. "I can see why a lot of people might want to kill Daphne DuBois. They revere her – you can see that – but they also fear her. There's some hate rolling around when she's not looking, too."

"Yeah, I picked up on the hate." Rowan made a bold move and slipped her foot over Quinn's ankle, resting her bare skin against his.

Quinn grinned when he saw the move, but he didn't comment. "Did you talk to any of the women this afternoon?"

"I talked to as many of them as I could. I wanted to see if anyone knew anything about Penny, but ironically enough, whenever conversation on Penny began it ultimately turned to a discussion about Daphne."

"How come?" Quinn moved his other foot on top of Rowan's ankle, smirking when she widened her eyes.

"Because Penny is Daphne's assistant."

"It has to be more than that," Quinn argued. "These women obviously associate Penny with Daphne on a personal level. Either they're friends – which I don't tend to believe because Daphne talked to Penny as if she were a slave when I was with them this afternoon – or Penny gossips behind Daphne's back and these other women now associate Penny with Daphne complaints."

"That's fairly solid thinking there." Rowan screwed up her face in concentration, making a face Quinn found utterly adorable. "I don't know what to do other than watch Penny."

"We can't watch her twenty-four hours a day," Quinn pointed out. "We saw how well that worked last time. We run the risk of people thinking we're stalkers."

"Or, in your case, we run the risk of the women thinking you're open for offers."

"And we don't want that." Quinn's smile doubled in size when Rowan rested her other foot on top of his. Their ankles now formed a weird pretzel. It was ridiculously silly and yet he couldn't muster the energy to care.

"We definitely don't want that because Daphne has decided that she wants you for herself."

Quinn's smile slipped. "That woman bothers me. She's extremely bossy and full of herself."

"You'd have to be to run a company, right?"

"Yeah, but she clearly doesn't understand what the word humility means," Quinn argued. "There are different ways to exert control – friendlier ones – and she clearly doesn't want to go that route."

"So ... what do we do?"

"We keep our eyes and ears open." Quinn extended his hand. "We also take a walk."

"A walk?"

Quinn nodded. "I want to take a walk with you. Even though we've talked, I feel as if I haven't seen you all day. We can continue making plans while we walk."

"It's raining," Rowan pointed out. "We'll get wet."

"Do you melt when you get wet?"

Rowan shook her head. "You run the risk of my hair turning into a big mass of uncontrollable curls given the humidity, though. You might mistake me for a witch in the wrong light."

"I can live with that." Quinn was reluctant to untangle his feet from Rowan's, but he was anxious to get some air. They'd earned a number of curious stares from fellow co-workers as they passed the table and Quinn felt as if he was on display.

"Okay." Rowan stood carefully to make sure she didn't

trip over Quinn's legs and shoved her phone in her pocket before taking his hand. "I don't want to hear one complaint about my hair when it grows to the size of a kraken, though."

Quinn barked out a laugh, genuinely amused. "I'm sure I'll be able to control my tongue."

The deck was quiet when they stepped out from the cover of the hallway, the night quiet other than a few scurrying guests who were anxious to avoid the rain. Since dinner was in full swing, Quinn wasn't overly worried about Penny expiring during their walk, figuring she was otherwise engaged and in the middle of a crowd.

"What are we going to do about dinner?" Rowan asked, lifting her face to the sky so she could feel the rain. She'd opted against wearing makeup because the humidity made her skin blotchy and Quinn couldn't help but marvel how pretty she was despite the lack of artificial manipulation.

"We can grab something at the deck restaurant in a little bit."

"Are we cleared to eat there?"

"I'm cleared to eat everywhere," Quinn replied. "I can also bring a date, so you're cleared to eat wherever I feel like eating."

"That's ... convenient."

"I think so." Quinn squeezed her hand as they walked, the couple falling into amiable silence. Thankfully the rain consisted of a light pattering rather than a steady deluge. It was more sprinkles than anything else.

As they walked, Rowan knew she should bring up Penny's safety and the shifting death omen. She was fairly certain the fact that the symbol hopped between individuals was significant. She had no idea why, though.

"Did you ever picture yourself living at sea half the

time?" Quinn asked, drawing Rowan toward the railing and slipping behind her so he could wrap his arms around her waist. The stance felt natural, as if Rowan should live there all of the time. He couldn't help but marvel about how comfortable he felt with her despite only knowing her for a few weeks.

"Not really." Rowan's lips curved as she ran her fingertips over Quinn's knuckles, which he had wrapped around the banister, essentially trapping her in place. "I'm always up for a new adventure, though. It's not as if I have anything holding me in Michigan. My family is gone for the most part, so ... I was kind of eager to come here."

"Still, you must wish you had family to anchor you."

"I wish for things that I can't change," Rowan clarified. "I wish my mother didn't die when I was a kid. I wish my father didn't follow her when I was barely an adult. I wish I knew what happened to my father so I could stop imagining so many terrible things."

"Yeah, not knowing is worse." Quinn rubbed his cheek against Rowan's as he stared at the rolling ocean. "When I was overseas, we hit a roadside bomb one day and I lost consciousness in the carnage. When I woke up, two of my fellow marines were dead, but a third was missing."

Rowan jerked her head to the side so she could study his profile. "Did you ever find him?"

Quinn shook his head. "I was confused. I had a concussion and a bad cut on my leg. When reinforcements arrived I was too out of it to issue orders. By the time I got my head on straight it was far too late to mount a search."

"What do you think happened?"

"I think he was probably injured and hurt like me but managed to get on his feet," Quinn answered, his voice strained. "I think he tried to go for help and headed in the wrong direction. He either died in the desert or was taken captive. I'm not sure which outcome is worse."

"In theory, he could still be alive."

"That was five years ago. If he was still alive and being held prisoner he probably wishes he was dead. Trust me. Sometimes dead is better."

Rowan mutely nodded, her heart going out to him. She wrapped her fingers around his and squeezed, at a loss for what to say. Thankfully Quinn saved her from the ordeal, shaking himself out of his reverie and gracing her with a small smile.

"I love walking in the rain," he volunteered. "I have since I was a kid. I love storms, too, although they're not a lot of fun at sea. When I'm on land, though, I like nothing better than sitting in a chair and watching a storm rage."

"I like storms, too," Rowan admitted. "I like putting horror movies on when they hit, though."

"You're an odd woman."

"Something tells me you like that."

"Something tells me you're right." Quinn shifted his face so his lips were inches from Rowan's. He had an opening – finally! – and he intended to use it. He lowered his mouth, his lips practically grazing hers, and then a petrified scream split the night air.

Quinn jerked back his head, eliciting a disappointed groan. He didn't have a chance to dwell on the lost chance, though, because another scream assailed his ears and he found himself running in the direction of the noise before he could register what almost happened.

Rowan followed closely at his heels, confused. Her heart pounded due to her proximity with Quinn a few moments before while her head reeled with worry because of the screaming.

Quinn pulled up short when he caught sight of a

flailing figure next to the railing at the aft side of the ship. He recognized Daphne DuBois right away. She had her hand pressed to the spot over her heart and she looked deranged as she swiveled her head from side to side.

"What's going on?" Quinn asked, stepping forward and catching Daphne's eye.

"Someone tried to kill me," Daphne gasped, taking two lurching steps away from the railing and throwing her arms around Quinn's neck.

Quinn caught her out of reflex, his skin recoiling at the woman's touch. Duty outweighed dislike, however, and he didn't attempt to dislodge her. "How did they try to kill you?"

"They tried to throw me over the deck." Daphne buried her face in Quinn's neck and clung to him. "I didn't see a face, although I'm pretty sure it was a woman. A big woman, mind you, but a woman all the same. I swear I smelled perfume. It was a very cheap perfume, if that helps."

"What happened?" Rowan asked, swallowing her dislike of Daphne.

"She came out of the darkness," Daphne replied. "She had a hood over her face and I couldn't see who she was. She took me by surprise and I opened my mouth to say something but … it was too late. She ran at me and tried to throw me over the railing."

"Where is she now?" Quinn asked, glancing around. He hadn't seen a hint of movement from anyone other than Daphne when he rounded the corner.

"She took off when I screamed," Daphne replied. "Oh, my heavens! I almost died! This is just the worst thing to happen ever." The woman tightened her arms around Quinn's neck and burst into hysterical tears. "What is this world coming to? I'm lucky to be alive. It's a miracle."

Six

Daphne was such a mess that she refused to release Quinn when more security details arrived. Despite his best efforts, Quinn found himself entangled. He could've sworn Daphne had at least eight of them given how many times she caught him during potential escape attempts.

Eventually Rowan offered a smile and curt nod, saying she was going to retire for the evening before shuffling off. Quinn watched her go, anger coursing through him. In his head he knew he shouldn't be angry with Daphne. She seemed legitimately upset, although she was obviously playing to a certain crowd once she realized she was drawing an audience. In his heart, though, Quinn couldn't help but curse the woman for her theatrics. If she'd waited thirty seconds – even ten seconds, for crying out loud – he would've been able to kiss Rowan. He had a feeling he would feel much better about Daphne's octopus Olympics if he had that memory to cherish.

"I think we've done everything we can for the night," Quinn said, taking a step away from Daphne. "You should probably return to your room and have a drink or something to settle your nerves. Everything will be better in the morning."

"Better?" Daphne arched an incredulous eyebrow. "Someone tried to kill me. How are things going to get better?"

Quinn stared back, unblinking. "Well, you won't be dead."

Daphne rolled her eyes. "I'll have business cards printed up with that on them. It will be my new motto."

"Whatever floats your boat." Quinn stepped to the side and focused on one of his men. "I want regular rounds on this deck twenty-four hours a day. I want one man on each side making regular passes. Come up with a schedule."

The man nodded. "I'll email you as soon as we're done, sir."

"Great." Quinn turned to leave, but Daphne grabbed his wrist before he could. He was almost at the limit of his patience and he had to bite the inside of his cheek to keep from lashing out at her. "Do you need something?"

"Do I need something? Of course I need something."

"Who are you talking to when you repeat my questions back to me like that?" Quinn challenged, snark winning out.

"I'm talking to you." Daphne's voice was firm as she smoothed her hair. Despite everything – a struggle to stay on deck when someone was trying to throw her overboard, a steady amount of rain – her hair remained perfectly coiffed.

"Ms. DuBois, it's getting late," Quinn pointed out. "I need to fill out some paperwork on the incident and then I want to turn in early because I'm sure I will have meetings regarding what happened first thing tomorrow morning."

"I understand that you have a job to do," Daphne sniffed. "It's just ... I'm very unsettled. I was hoping you could walk me back to my room and … I don't know … sit with me a bit."

Quinn's eyebrows winged up his forehead. That was the last thing he wanted to do. "Sit with you?"

Daphne widened her eyes and blinked rapidly, as if she was trying to muster tears. "I'm afraid. You're the head of security. I think the only way I'll feel safe is if you're with me … all night."

She threw in that last part as if it were some sort of bonus. Quinn was done messing around, however. He calmly extricated his arm from her grip, extended a warning finger when she moved to grab him again, and firmly shook his head.

"Ma'am, I understand you've had a trying experience tonight and I don't want to belittle that." Quinn chose his words carefully and adopted a stern face. "The fact remains that I have a job to do. I cannot let you interfere with that job.

"Now, if you're truly afraid, I can have one of my men position himself outside your door this evening," he continued. "It would be unprofessional for that man to be in your room, however, so you'll have to make do with your own company or that of one of your workers." That wasn't exactly true, but Quinn didn't want to unjustly punish one of his employees, and he could think of nothing worse than being trapped in a tiny room with Daphne DuBois.

"I have paperwork that has to be filed," Quinn added. "I have things that have to be attended to tomorrow. I'm sorry that you're frightened and feel uneasy regarding your surroundings – I truly am – but I cannot sit with you all night."

"Fine." Daphne's eyes filled with fire. "Do whatever you need to do. Far be it from me to stand in your way."

"That's my plan, ma'am." Quinn ignored her tone –

and murderous expression – as he turned away from her. He was only a few feet away when he was forced to pull up short because he saw Demarcus watching the scene with unveiled amusement. "This is hardly funny."

"I think that depends on which direction you're coming from," Demarcus countered. "From where I'm at, well, this is downright hilarious."

"I'm glad you're having a good time." Quinn ran a frustrated hand over the top of his short-cropped hair as he glanced around the deck. "This is so weird. I don't know what to think."

Demarcus widened his eyes, surprised. "Do you think she's making it up?" He kept his voice low. "I wouldn't put it past her given all of the stories I've heard."

"I'm actually curious about those stories, but I'm going to have to wait until tomorrow morning to listen to them," Quinn said, sighing. "I don't suppose you've seen Rowan, have you?"

"She went back to her cabin."

"I know but ... ."

"You thought she might wait out here for you?" Demarcus' eyes twinkled. "Does your heart hurt because she didn't wait for you?"

"My heart *does* hurt," Quinn confirmed. "Not because of that, though." He exhaled heavily through his nose as he tried to center himself. "This entire thing sucks. It's weird ... I hate these women ... and I really wish I could've finished my walk with Rowan instead of dealing with this. I know that sounds selfish given the circumstances but ... there it is."

Demarcus didn't bother to hide his mirth. "I don't blame you. That brings me back to my previous question, though. Do you think she faked the attack?"

Quinn shrugged, unsure how to answer. "Let's just say

I'm not completely believing her story and leave it at that for now."

"Got it." Demarcus mock-saluted. "So what are you going to do?"

"File some paperwork and go to bed. There's not much else I can do."

"Okay, well … I'm sorry your date with Rowan got cut short."

"It wasn't technically a date," Quinn argued. "It was, however, a lost opportunity. If I don't kiss her soon I swear I'm going to rip someone's face off. Right now, Daphne DuBois has the unfortunate honor of being the person I want to do that to because she totally ruined my chance."

Instead of laughing like Quinn envisioned, Demarcus opened his mouth and quietly worked his jaw. The gesture was enough to make Quinn unnaturally defensive. "What?"

"You haven't kissed her yet?" Demarcus was incredulous.

Quinn jolted at the question and looked around to see if anyone was listening. "Do you mind keeping your voice down?"

"What is the matter with you? You're straight, right?"

Quinn scowled. "What is the matter with you? My kissing habits are none of your business."

"Apparently they're none of anyone's business." Demarcus leaned forward conspiratorially. "Do you need some tips to seal the deal? I can probably help you if you're desperate."

"Oh, that did it!" Quinn threw his hands up in the air and stormed away from a chuckling Demarcus. He knew the man was messing with him, but the jabs hit close to home.

"Say hello to Rowan for me," Demarcus called to his

back. "Actually … don't say anything at all. The second she opens the door, plant one on her. You're a manly man. Remember that."

"Thanks, Demarcus. I've got it." Quinn didn't bother turning around.

Sally, who had been loitering in the shadows during the discussion, stepped out and fixed Demarcus with a pointed look. "I thought we agreed to let them work things out on their own."

"We did." Demarcus was sheepish. "The boy needs help, though. He's stumbling all over himself."

Sally sighed. "Fine. Don't make a habit of it, though. It will be more special if they stumble through this messy game of life on their own terms."

"I'm not sure how much fun that will be for Rowan."

"Yes, well … ." Sally let her eyes drift toward the door Quinn disappeared through. "He really hasn't kissed her yet? Rowan left that part out of our discussion the other day."

"It took me by surprise, too. I thought he would be good at the kissing part."

"Just because he hasn't kissed her yet doesn't mean he's not good at it," Sally admonished. "He could be a savant or something, for all we know."

"He'd better be," Demarcus muttered. "If I had to wait for two weeks to get my first kiss, I don't care who it was, I'd be expecting a transfer of diamonds with the saliva."

Sally made a disgusted face. "You're kind of a gross guy. You know that, right?"

Demarcus shrugged. "The fact that you're just figuring that out means you don't know me at all."

. . .

QUINN HAD a full head of steam when he knocked on Rowan's door. He could hear her shuffling on the other side and he puffed out his chest when she pulled open the door. He was ready to grab her and follow his instincts before she had a chance to utter one word. Then, despite his best intentions, he deflated.

"Is something wrong?"

Rowan was dressed in a pair of cotton sleep pants, a tank top, and reading glasses. Her long auburn hair was pulled back in a messy bun on top of her head. She looked utterly ... vulnerable. That was the only word Quinn could think of to describe her.

Rowan self-consciously covered her braless chest with her arms as Quinn struggled to find the right words. "Did something happen?"

"What? No." Quinn shook his head. "I just ... you left without saying goodbye."

"I said goodbye," Rowan countered, pushing open the door so Quinn could step inside. She didn't think having this discussion in the hallway would be conducive to her determination to remain out of the ship's gossip mill. "I just couldn't get close when I said it. Daphne wasn't afraid to throw elbows if anyone dared approach and I didn't want to risk a black eye."

Quinn sighed, weariness overtaking him. "I'm sorry about that. I'm sorry about everything. That's not how I saw our night going."

"It's okay." Rowan appeared nervous as she perched on the end of her bed. "We both have jobs to do while we're here. It's hard because we're technically living our jobs, but we have a lot of down time and we can generally spend whatever amount of that time we choose together. This was just one of those fluke things that forced us to take a different course."

"Yeah? Well, it seems like this 'fluke' thing is going to be a 'pain in the butt' thing tomorrow," Quinn said, shuffling closer to Rowan. "Daphne tried to get me to spend the night in her room with her."

Rowan's previously sleepy eyes flew open. "Excuse me?"

"She said she was afraid and needed me to sit with her." Quinn saw no reason to lie and he refused to hold anything back where Rowan was concerned. "I explained I had a job to do and that wouldn't happen and she didn't take it well."

"What's 'not well'?"

"She gave me attitude and pouted a bit," Quinn answered. "I didn't hang around long enough to see if she was going to make a scene. I needed to get away from her so I left my guys to handle it."

Rowan's lips curved. "Way to delegate authority."

"I thought so."

Unlike before when they were on the deck, the silence that shrouded the couple this time was decidedly uncomfortable. Quinn grasped for something – anything, really – to ease the tension. "What did you do while I was busy with Daphne?"

"Oh, well … ." Rowan rolled to the side so Quinn would have room to sit and she gestured toward her computer. "These are the photos I took today. Now, I'm not happy because so many of them are staged, but I'm not the boss. I prefer candid shots. Daphne? Yeah, not so much. She has already marked a hundred of them for purchase."

"A hundred of them, huh?" Quinn shifted his eyes to the computer, relieved to have a reason to stay. "What am I looking at?"

"Women hanging around together."

"Okay, I guess the better question is, why are you looking at this?"

"Do you notice anything odd about them?" Rowan asked, her eyes locked on Quinn's face rather than the screen. "I'm not trying to trick you or anything. I honestly need you to give them a good look."

"Okay." Quinn exhaled shakily, the scent of Rowan's simple body spray causing his chest to constrict. After a few moments of quiet perusal, he lost himself in the photos. He was fairly certain he knew what Rowan was getting at before she opened her mouth. "Daphne positions herself in the center of every single photo."

"Every one," Rowan agreed, bobbing her head. "She's like the Beyonce of Cara G Cosmetics. She always has to put herself in front of everyone else. We're not the only ones to notice, either. Look here ... and here ... and here."

"Yeah, I see what you mean," Quinn said. "She's getting dirty looks from the women she's standing in front of. You said she'd ordered a bunch of copies, right? She has to have noticed this."

"That's what I'm wondering." Rowan chewed on her bottom lip, conflicted. "I don't want to cast stones or point fingers but ... um ... do you think Daphne was really attacked?"

"Believe it or not, you're not the first person to ask me that." Quinn rolled his neck until it cracked. "I'm going to tell you exactly what I told Demarcus: I honestly don't know. I don't want to jump to conclusions right out of the gate because that hardly seems fair, but we should've seen or heard something on that deck before Daphne screamed. I mean ... how did someone get past us and escape like that?"

"At least I'm not the only one thinking it," Rowan

murmured. "I felt guilty, kept wondering if maybe I was jealous and that's why I thought the worst of her."

"Jealous?" Quinn tilted his head to the side. "Why would you be jealous?"

"I know I shouldn't be," Rowan clarified. "I just couldn't seem to stop myself. Whenever I saw her touching you I kind of wanted to throw her over the railing myself."

Quinn snickered. "I'm going to let you in on a little secret, Trixie. I wanted to toss her over as well. Her very presence irked the crap out of me."

"Oh, I'm so relieved." Rowan rested her hand on top of his. "I'm not evil alone. I can't tell you how much better that makes me feel."

Quinn snickered, genuinely amused. "Yeah." He flipped over Rowan's hand, linking their fingers together as he raised their joined hands and brushed a kiss against her knuckles. "Hey, Rowan?"

"What?" Her voice was breathy and Quinn knew she understood what was about to come. He explained anyway.

"I'm about to kiss you," Quinn volunteered. "I really need to do it because otherwise I might die. I know that sounds dramatic, but that's how I feel. Okay, I probably won't die. I might pass out or kick someone because I'm in a bad mood, though."

"I ... okay." Rowan's mouth went dry.

"Okay?"

Rowan bobbed her head. "Okay."

Quinn leaned forward and smiled, pausing when his lips were so close to Rowan's face that she could feel nothing but his warm breath against her lips and chin. "I've wanted to do this since the moment I met you."

"Me, too."

"Something always gets in the way ... and I'm sorry for that."

Rowan was out of patience. She took both of them by surprise when she grabbed the sides of his face. "No more talking." She smacked her lips against his, sinking into the kiss when his arms came around her.

They mashed their lips together for what seemed like forever, Quinn losing track of where his mouth ended and hers began. When they finally parted, both of them gasping for breath, Quinn cupped the back of her head as he stared into her eyes.

"I'm going to need to do that again," Quinn gritted out.

"Good." Rowan was done being meek. "I think we should make a schedule if you think you're going to get shy again all of a sudden. That way you have to do it if it's on the schedule."

"Screw your schedule," Quinn said, tugging Rowan closer. "I'm pretty sure the shyness is over."

"It had better be."

"Shh. Kiss me."

"No, you kiss me!"

In the end they kissed each other ... absolutely senseless.

Seven

Rowan woke to Quinn sleeping peacefully beside her. He spent the night, although they didn't go further than kissing. That seemed to be enough for both of them and when they finally slipped under – well after midnight – they both slept hard.

As if sensing her stirring, Quinn opened one eye and slipped an arm around her waist, tugging her closer. "Go back to sleep."

"It's almost eight. I have to hit the employee dining room by nine if I want breakfast."

"They serve breakfast in the main dining room until ten," he reminded her. "You're allowed to eat in the main dining room. It's part of your contract because you take photos there. It's fine. If anyone has a problem, have them take it up with me."

Rowan snorted as she moved her thumb over his bottom lip. They kissed so long and so hard his mouth almost looked swollen. "Are you going to fight all of my battles for me now?"

"Just the important ones." Quinn brushed a kiss over

her forehead. "We were up late and it's going to be a long day. Go back to sleep for at least an hour."

Rowan wanted to argue. She was being paid to do a job, after all. Still, he looked so comfortable, content even. "One hour. I have to be at the Cara G Cosmetics conference for the bulk of the afternoon. It's not all fun and games for the ladies while they're here."

"Yeah, I saw the schedule." Quinn drew the blanket closer around Rowan's back. "They have three hours of conference time every afternoon. I have no idea how someone can fill that much time talking about makeup but … whatever. Close your eyes."

"They're closed."

"Shut down your mind."

"I'm working on it."

"Give me another kiss."

"Okay, but my lips are actually sore."

"Some things are worth the pain, Rowan. I'm pretty sure this is one of those things."

Rowan was fairly certain he was right.

TWO HOURS later Rowan wiped the corners of her mouth and stared ruefully at her empty breakfast plate. She didn't think she was hungry until she devoured a full omelet, hash browns, two servings of toast, and three glasses of tomato juice.

"I think I ate too much." She rubbed her stomach as she caught Quinn's amused gaze across the table. "Why did you let me eat so much?"

"I didn't know I was your food monitor. It's okay. I like a woman with a little meat on her bones."

Rowan stilled. "Meat?" She glanced down at her

thighs, earning a harsh look from Quinn. "Um, I should probably get going."

"Hold on a second." Quinn caught her hand before she could scurry away from the table. "That was a poor joke. You look beautiful. You always look beautiful. I guess I forgot that women take things like that to heart. I won't make that mistake again."

"I didn't take it to heart," Rowan said hurriedly. "I just ... am running late."

"Yeah, I don't believe you, but we'll talk about it later." Quinn grunted as he got to his feet, rearranging the waistband of his shorts. "Speaking of that, though, why did you let me eat so much?"

Despite her earlier discomfort, Rowan couldn't stop herself from giggling. "Maybe we both needed the calories after last night."

"Maybe." Quinn pressed a light kiss to Rowan's lips. "I hate to say it, but my lips are sore."

"I told you."

"Yes, well, when you're right, you're right." Quinn rubbed his hands up and down Rowan's bare arms. "I'm spending the rest of my morning in my office finishing up paperwork. I'll look for you when the conference ends. You should have eyes on Penny throughout the entire afternoon, right?"

Rowan solemnly nodded. "I'll watch her and Daphne."

"Be careful when you're doing it. We don't want either of them getting paranoid because they think we're watching them. In Daphne's case, that could backfire in a way neither one of us is comfortable dealing with."

"If either of them leaves the room, I'll text you."

"That sounds like a plan." Quinn spared time for one more kiss and then released Rowan. "Be careful."

"I'm not in danger."

"Be careful anyway."

Rowan added a little swing to her step as she left, something that didn't escape Quinn's attention. He was still smiling when he felt a presence move up on his right side.

"I see you finally handled that kissing problem," Demarcus noted, enjoying the way Quinn's mouth tipped down at the corners. "How did the rest of it go?"

"I'm not talking to you about any of this," Quinn shot back, wagging a finger as he swiveled. "You have a big mouth and if you think I don't know you're at the center of the bulk of the ship's gossip, you're wrong."

"I never claimed to be a pure soul. I love my gossip." Demarcus solemnly lifted his chin. "What tidbits do you have to share with the Gossipfather."

It took Quinn a moment to realize Demarcus was making a joke about *The Godfather*. When he grasped the statement, he didn't bother hiding his chuckle. "You're incorrigible. I already told you that I'm not sharing information with you."

"Fine. Be that way." Demarcus heaved out a long-suffering sigh. "You know that Rowan is going to confide in Sally and she, in turn, will confide in me, right? You're not saving yourself from the Gossipfather. You're only delaying the inevitable."

"I can live with that." Quinn clapped Demarcus on the shoulder as he passed. "By the way, do me a favor and keep an eye on the chief makeup chick, will you?"

"Daphne DuBois?" Demarcus' demeanor shifted quickly. "Do you think someone is after her?"

"I'm still on the fence." Quinn opted for honesty. "There's something about her story that doesn't make sense. That doesn't mean the bulk of it isn't true. Someone very well may have tried to chuck her overboard. Perhaps Daphne knows who that is and is covering to save face."

"Ah, a pink coup."

"It's not out of the realm of possibility," Quinn acknowledged. "The one thing that I've found most of these women agree on is the fact that they don't like Daphne. If someone did try to off her, I'm worried we're dealing with an extensive suspect pool."

Demarcus shifted his eyes so he could absorb the pink sea in the dining room. "You've got that right, buddy. I'll keep my eyes and ears open, though."

"Thank you. It's nice to know that you'll use your powers for good instead of evil today."

"Oh, don't kid yourself." Mischief lit Demarcus' eyes. "I'm going to do both. I will find out what you and Rowan Gray did in her room last night … and before you deny it, I know you didn't spend the night in your own room."

Quinn saw no reason to confirm or deny the statement. "I'll be around if you find anything."

"And I'll be around if you feel the sudden need to unburden yourself."

ROWAN SPENT the better part of the next three hours on her feet, loitering in the back of the large conference hall as Daphne DuBois and her executive team ran the world's most boring event. Rowan knew she was probably being petty because she wasn't thrilled with Daphne's interest in Quinn, but not even the omen shadow hanging over Penny Parker was enough to make time move faster for the intrepid photographer.

By the time Daphne finished up, unleashing a rousing speech about how the women weren't selling a product but themselves, Rowan had to stifle a series of yawns and make herself small in the back of the room when Daphne caught her doing it.

Rowan was hopeful she would be able to escape without talking to Daphne. She didn't get that lucky.

"Ms. Gray, might I have a word?"

Rowan cringed when she heard the voice, removing her thumb from the photo slide at the back of her camera and forcing a smile as she swiveled. "Of course. Did I miss something during your presentation?"

"Oh, no, I'm sure you got everything that was important." Daphne gestured toward the nearby table. It was empty, the women who sat there during the conference practically fleeing from the room the second Daphne finished her spiel. "I thought we might have a talk."

That didn't sound good. Rowan refused to show reticence when meeting Daphne's gaze, though. Instead she widened her smile and dutifully sat. "What do you want to talk about?"

"Last night."

Rowan stilled, confused. *Was Daphne DuBois really going to question her about Quinn spending the night in her room?* "I'm not sure what you're getting at, but I'm fairly certain this is a conversation we shouldn't be having."

"Because you're not allowed to speak ill about your employer?"

Now Rowan was doubly confused. "Why would I speak ill about my employer?"

"Because he's created an unsafe work environment," Daphne replied, not missing a beat. "I was attacked and almost thrown overboard while visiting a ship whose owners boast about having top notch security. I hardly think that's the case, do you?"

Something about Daphne's tone set Rowan's teeth on edge. "Are you thinking of filing a formal complaint about the security? If so, I can promise you that no one was negligent. Mr. Davenport ran to your aid the moment he knew something was amiss."

"Oh, I'm not complaining about Mr. Davenport." Daphne gave the suggestion a dismissive wave. "He seems competent, if distracted." Her gaze was pointed when it landed on Rowan. "No, Mr. Davenport isn't the problem. I will, of course, request a change to that pesky rule about keeping security outside of guest rooms. That's just nonsense. I expect to have that tossed within the hour, though, so it's a very minor complaint."

"You do?" Rowan briefly wondered if she should warn Quinn about Daphne's plans.

"I do." Daphne bobbed her head. "That's not the issue, though. This ship is the issue. It's hardly safe for a woman to walk the decks when she can be tossed over-board at any moment."

"I'm not sure how to respond to that." Rowan kept her voice even as she attempted to figure out exactly what Daphne was getting at. "Do you want to cover the ship in plastic wrap – or perhaps a bubble – to make sure there's no danger of someone inadvertently going over the side?"

"That's an intriguing thought, but that would probably ruin the ambiance." Daphne rubbed a well-manicured finger over her cheek. "I was thinking more about having security guards stationed every twenty feet along the railing to make sure that there's absolutely no way anyone could fall to their death – whether by accident or intent."

Daphne had a hoity-toity way of talking that Rowan didn't particularly like. "I see. Well, that would entail putting a guard on every single balcony, too, since they look out on the open sea. I doubt very much that the company is going to foot the bill for that. Plus, well, the privacy issues would be profound."

"I hadn't thought of that," Daphne mused. "It's a good point and yet ... well ... I almost died last night. Perhaps if you almost died you would have a different take on matters."

"Perhaps," Rowan readily agreed. "I think you're safe as long as you don't wander the deck alone, though. I'm sure whoever came after you wouldn't have bothered if you weren't hanging out alone. I'm not saying it's your fault, mind you, just that you should take added precautions while you're on the ship. You know, just to be on the safe side."

"Yes, well, I already have a plan to make sure that doesn't happen again," Daphne said. "In fact, I have a meeting with the captain in twenty minutes and that's exactly what we're going to discuss."

"Michael?" Rowan knit her eyebrows. She'd only met Michael Griffin a few times. The man had a reputation as something of a sex machine and serial groper, so Rowan went out of her way to give him a wide berth. Quinn swore up and down that the reputation was exaggerated, but Rowan wasn't taking any chances. "Well, he's a nice man. I'm sure you'll have a pleasant chat with one another."

"I think we will, too," Daphne said breezily. "I'm going to ask him to lift the rule about security guards keeping watch in guest rooms overnight and then I'm going to make sure Mr. Davenport is close to watch my back for the remainder of my stay. I think that's the only thing that will make me feel safe."

"Oh, um ... hmm." Rowan had no idea what to say to that so she pressed her mouth shut and stared at her feet. Part of her wanted to call Daphne on her attitude, but no matter how things went, Rowan knew she would come out of that scenario looking like the bad guy given Daphne's terrible ordeal the night before.

"Does that bother you?" Daphne locked gazes with Rowan. "I mean … is there a reason Mr. Davenport shouldn't spend the night in my room?"

Rowan wanted to answer that Quinn would be spending the night in her room, but she didn't know if that was actually the case. He stayed close the night before because they both needed it. They'd made no further plans on what was to come. "I think Mr. Davenport is capable of making his own decisions."

"Yes, but … rumor has it that you two might be making decisions together now."

Rumor has it? Rowan didn't bother to hide her irritation. "I didn't realize you were keyed in to the ship's gossip mill. Do you have something specific you want to ask?"

"I like a woman who puts her cards on the table." Daphne's smile was serene. "You would do well in cosmetic sales, once you clean up your complexion and learn how to apply eyeliner in the proper manner, of course."

"Of course."

"As for the rest, I guess I'll come right out and ask it," Daphne pressed. "Are you and Mr. Davenport involved?"

"Yes." Rowan refused to lie.

"I see." Daphne clearly didn't like the answer. She folded her fingers together and primly rested them on her lap. "Is this a monogamous relationship?"

"We haven't gotten that far."

"Meaning?"

Rowan bit down on her bottom lip to keep herself from saying something harsh. She counted to ten, sucked in a breath, and then forced a smile. "Meaning that it's a new thing for both of us."

"So … he's not your boyfriend?"

"You'll have to ask him that."

"I'm asking you."

"I don't know if he's my boyfriend because we haven't talked about it." Rowan pushed herself to a standing position and grabbed her camera from the table. "Now, if you'll excuse me, this is a wildly unprofessional conversation and I have work to do."

"Yes, well, go back to your work." Daphne made shooing motions with her fingers. "I'll handle everything else."

Rowan wanted to ask what the woman meant by that, but she was afraid her temper would get the better of her and either she or Daphne would end up with a powder puff to the face (and possibly a mascara brush to the eye) if she didn't leave right now.

"Good luck with that," Rowan gritted out. "I'll have the photos from the conference uploaded within the next few hours."

"I'm looking forward to seeing them."

Eight

"Absolutely not."

Quinn planted his hands on his hips and vehemently shook his head to cut off Captain Michael Griffin before he even finished his request. He knew the moment the man called him into his office that there was going to be trouble.

"I haven't even gotten to the question yet," Michael complained, glaring. "Don't you think I've earned the right to finish my question?"

"Sure." Quinn bobbed his head even though his expression remained immovable.

"Daphne DuBois has requested that you spend the night in her room to protect her."

"Absolutely not."

"Okay, well, I asked." Michael's grin was cheeky as he gestured toward the chair across from his desk. "She's not going to like the answer, but I told her that there was no way I would force an employee to do something like that. I can't wait to tell her. Oh, wait, I can wait."

"I'll tell her." Quinn's temper bubbled toward the surface as he sank into the chair. "I'm legitimately looking forward to telling her. I think it's going to be the highlight of my day." His mind flashed to waking up with Rowan. "Or maybe the second best part of my day."

"Are you going to be pleasant when you tell her?"

"No."

Michael made a face. "You know that I hear it from the higher-ups when you mouth off to the guests, right? It's not fun."

"That woman is the devil."

"She could very well be the devil," Michael agreed. "She sashayed in here and pasted this fake smile on her face ... and this was after she demanded a meeting even though I said I was busy. She used this really friendly tone of voice and then proceeded to talk down to me like I was an idiot."

"Why didn't you shut her down there?" Quinn was genuinely curious.

"Because this cruise is a yearly thing and it brings in a lot of money," Michael replied. "Listen, I'm only going to put up with so much crap, but I didn't see the harm in asking. I explained I couldn't force you to do anything and that I didn't foresee you agreeing to her suggestion, but she didn't believe me."

"Really?" Quinn rolled his neck until it cracked. "She has a unique sense of self. I have to give her that. I could've sworn on a stack of Bibles that she had eight arms last night. That's how active she was trying to hold onto me."

"You made your escape, though, didn't you?"

"I certainly did."

"I understand you made your escape to a certain photographer's room." Michael's eyes sparkled. "How did that go?"

"Oh, geez." Quinn pinched the bridge of his nose to

ward off a potential headache. "Have you been spending time with Demarcus?"

"He is the best bartender on the ship."

"Yes, well, he's also a gossipy pain in the butt."

"I can live with that."

Quinn sighed, the sound heavy and hollow. In truth, Michael was probably the best friend he had on the Bounding Storm. They didn't spend a lot of time together – and Michael had no interest in following Quinn around to force social interaction – but they were still fairly close. "It was fine," he gritted out after a beat.

"Fine?"

"That's what I said."

"Demarcus said you spent the night and came out looking all sloppy and happy."

"Demarcus is going to get a boot in the rear end before the day is out," Quinn shot back.

"Oh, come on." Michael didn't bother hiding his mirth. "You've been panting after that woman since you first saw her. You've finally gotten her. Are we talking forever or for now?"

"We don't know each other all that well," Quinn replied, annoyed. "We're having a wonderful time, though."

"Oh, that was a pathetic answer. It was almost so diplomatic it was so boring." Michael made a clucking sound as he shook his head. "I expected more from you."

"Yeah?" Quinn came from a military background and while men were mostly respectful of women he would be lying if he said there wasn't the occasional off-color joke. He even made a few himself. He couldn't bring himself to offer anything like that where Rowan was concerned. "I like her."

"I know. I've seen you two together. You're in your own

little world even when you're simply sharing drinks and staring at the ocean."

"So why did you ask?"

"Because I was curious to see what you would say." Michael leaned back in his chair, steepling his fingers as he rested his elbows on his stomach. "It's okay to like her. You know that, right?"

"I know that. I have no problem admitting I like her. What I do have a problem with is the way the people who work on this ship won't stop staring. It's hard to date when you're the only fish in the bowl."

"That will ease eventually. You just have to give it a few days ... two weeks at the most."

"I hope so." Quinn flashed a genuine smile as he stood. "I'll track down Ms. DuBois and inform her of my decision. You don't have to worry about doing it yourself."

"That would be great. I'm going to hide here until she focuses her attention on someone else."

Quinn shook his head, legitimately amused. "You could always volunteer to stay with her."

"Oh, I'll never be that hard up. Did you see that hair? It's like a helmet."

"I saw it. I can't wait until I never have to see it again."

"Yes, well, speaking of helmets ... um ... you might want to wear a cup when you tell her you're bowing out," Michael suggested. "I have a feeling she kicks."

"I'll keep it in mind."

ROWAN WAS tired when she hit her room. Between three hours at the conference, an annoying conversation with Daphne, and then another two hours on deck under the unrelenting sun, she was ready to hit the shower.

Rowan never considered herself a jealous person until

Daphne practically slapped her across the face with a dueling glove and challenged her to fight for Quinn's affection. She had no intention of stooping to Daphne's level, but she also didn't want Quinn thinking she didn't care enough to muster the effort. It was an interesting conundrum.

Rowan was so lost in thought she didn't notice the single flower leaning against her door until she almost stepped on it. She widened her eyes, glancing around the empty hallway before leaning over to pick up the pink rose.

It was beautiful in its simplicity and Rowan pressed it to her nose to inhale the intoxicating scent. She'd seen the roses offered for purchase at one of the gift shops off the main lobby, the color selected specifically for the Cara G Cosmetics guests. There was no note attached, but Rowan was fairly certain she knew who sent it.

The first thing she did upon entering the room was find something to use as a vase. She had to settle for a tall glass, but she really didn't mind. Once she added water to the glass and stripped out of her clothes she headed straight for the shower.

Ten minutes before she'd been exhausted, briefly wondering if she should skip dinner in favor of a nap. Now all she could think about was dressing up in something nice and finding Quinn so they could share a meal together.

Her mood unbelievably uplifted, Rowan left her cell phone on the bed before disappearing into the bathroom. The night was looking up.

"THERE YOU ARE!"

Daphne, a fruity drink in her hand and a sarong hanging low on her hips as she danced back and forth in her bikini, fixed Quinn with a flirty smile as he approached her on the deck. It was almost five and Quinn couldn't help but wonder if the cosmetics dynamo planned to drink her supper. He honestly didn't care – or judge – but it would make things worse if the woman was drunk when he shot her down.

"Here I am," Quinn confirmed, sparing a glance at the group of Cara G Cosmetics representatives slurping drinks on pool loungers. "Do you have a minute to talk?"

"I've got a whole bunch of minutes for you," Daphne purred, puffing out her ample chest and causing the women to giggle in appreciation. "If you only need a minute, I'll be so disappointed. What do you want to talk about? I'm guessing it's about your sleeping arrangements tonight. You don't have to worry. There's plenty of room in my bed."

The gaggle of women let loose with a series of cat sounds, a few making claws with their hands and swiping them through the air.

"I know someone who is going to be having a good night," Penny intoned, beaming.

"Yes, I know someone who will be having a good night, too," Quinn said. "Can we talk, Ms. DuBois?"

"Call me Daphne."

"I'm fine calling you Ms. DuBois. It's more professional."

"Yes, but it's also cold." Daphne wrinkled her nose as she ran her finger down Quinn's chest. "You don't make me feel cold."

"I think you would prefer having this conversation in private," Quinn supplied, catching Daphne's hand and shoving it back. "I know I would."

Daphne stilled, her eyes momentarily shifting from flirty to murderous. She recovered quickly and plastered the familiar fake smile on her face. "Okay, well, do you have a specific location where you'd like to chat?"

"I'll bet he wants to chat in his bedroom," Penny teased.

"Over there will be fine." Quinn pointed to an empty spot in front of the railing.

"Okay, well, let's go." Daphne squared her shoulders as she moved in that direction. Quinn was secretly relieved that she didn't appear to be shaky on her feet. Once they were alone, Daphne swiveled and fixed Quinn with a blinding smile. "I never took you for being shy. If you're upset about the teasing, well, you don't have to worry. I know you'll be staying in my room to do a job ... nothing else. All that talk was simply my friends blowing off steam."

"I'm not staying in your room." Quinn was matter-of-fact. "That's not going to happen. It's not part of my job description. It's simply not how this night is going to go."

"But ... I talked to the captain."

"Who cannot make me do something I don't want to do. I can place a security representative outside of your room if that makes you feel better, but he will not be forced to spend the night in your room either."

"Forced? That's such a harsh word."

"Can you think of a better word?"

"Um ... how about want? Why don't you want to spend the night in my room? I'm a witty conversationalist."

"And I'm not interested." Quinn crossed his arms over his chest, giving off an air of authority and aloofness that couldn't possibly be mistaken for anything other than it was. "I am not some prize in a game you're playing. I'm not up for manipulation. I can't be bullied."

"I wasn't trying to bully you," Daphne protested, her

demeanor faltering. "I don't appreciate being talked to in this manner. I hope you know that."

"I don't really care." Quinn rolled his neck as weariness descended on his broad shoulders. "Please stop playing games because I've got a full schedule. I'm trying to figure out exactly who wanted to throw you off this ship. I'm guessing I have a lot of suspects to sift through."

"What's that supposed to mean?"

"Take it however you want," Quinn snapped. "I'm done messing around, though. If you have a legitimate security question, the door to my office is always open. Otherwise ... I'm busy."

Quinn turned on his heel and stalked toward the bar, the pressure in his chest lifting when he realized he'd tackled the hardest part of his day. Things could only get better from here on out. The feeling of euphoria only lasted a few seconds, right until Penny Parker stepped in front of him and cut off his avenue of escape.

"Now what?" he barked, immediately lifting his hands by way of apology when he noticed the way the woman jerked her shoulders. "I'm sorry. That was uncalled for."

"It's okay." Penny's voice was small and she took a moment to collect herself. "I didn't mean to bother you. It's just ... um ... I wanted to apologize for whatever it is that Daphne said to you. She doesn't always understand the way she comes off. She doesn't do the things she does on purpose."

"See, I'm going to part ways with you there. I think she knows exactly what she's doing. Like a typical bully, she gauges people. She wants to see how far she can push them before they push back. I can't be pushed at all without pushing back. That's the message I just conveyed to her."

"And she doesn't look happy about it," Penny noted, inclining her chin toward the lounger where Daphne dejectedly sat as she downed a huge drink. "She's going to be a bear tonight. She's been telling people all day that she's going to get to know you better."

"Well, she'll have to get used to disappointment." Quinn was purposely blasé. "I can't be manipulated and I don't like it when people try to force me into doing something I don't want to do."

"That's not really what she was doing," Penny countered. "She likes you. That's simply the way she shows it."

"She doesn't like me."

"She does."

"She doesn't even know me."

"Oh, well, she likes what she sees when she looks at you," Penny clarified. "She's honestly not a bad person. She's just … misunderstood."

Penny said the words, but Quinn didn't believe them for a second. When he looked at the younger woman he saw a person who was used to cleaning up her boss's mistakes. She was a sad individual who spent her time living someone else's life. "She's a pain in the butt," Quinn corrected. "It doesn't matter, though. I told her where things stand and she's going to have to deal with that."

"She won't be happy about it."

"I don't care."

"She'll make trouble for you," Penny warned, lowering her voice. "She'll go to your boss and make trouble for you because she thinks she needs to punish people who don't do everything she wants them to do. She can be brutal when she wants to be."

"I'm not worried about that. I have a contract. If my employers have a problem, they'll contact me. Just for the record, though, I would be willingly fired – heck, I would quit this job – rather than spend time with that woman."

Penny's mouth dropped open in surprise. "I … um … okay."

"Just so long as we're clear." Quinn forced a tight smile as he stepped around Penny. "Make sure she doesn't go anywhere alone. You're her assistant, right? Your biggest job now is to watch her."

"I'll do that."

"Good, because I really don't know anyone else who wants the job."

Nine

Quinn was in a fairly decent mood by the time he hit the main dining room. Penny's warning about her boss's potential machinations didn't worry him. He'd seen worse overseas. There was nothing a territorial cosmetics company president could do to frighten him. If Daphne DuBois wanted to cause problems she could call the head of the cruise liner company and file a complaint. Quinn refused to live in fear because of one petulant woman.

He scanned the dining room for Rowan. They'd chatted by text during the afternoon hours and agreed to meet in the dining room for dinner. In truth, Quinn would've been happy grabbing a couple plates of food and moving to the deck so they could have some time alone together. He was officially sick of people – especially people wearing the color pink – and he was more than ready for some solitude.

Quinn picked his way through the busy dining room, offering the occasional watery smile to Cara G Cosmetics representatives when they called out to him. For some reason his name was on everyone's lips, as if they'd all managed to hold a meeting when no one was looking and agreed to join together to torture him, and all he could do was offer a half-hearted wave as he cut his way through the crowd.

Demarcus worked behind the main bar counter, and when Quinn hoisted himself up on a stool the busy bartender spared an amused grin. He sensed Quinn's weariness and discomfort – and part of him was sympathetic to the man's plight – but the security guru's unease was too entertaining to ignore.

"I heard that the Bounding Storm is going to hire out your stud services for the rest of the cruise," Demarcus drawled, enjoying the way Quinn cringed and hunkered lower on his stool. "I think it's a fantastic idea. In ten months the world will be inundated with moody little kids threatening to punch everyone's lights out when they're angry. It's bound to be entertaining."

"Ha, ha," Quinn intoned, wrinkling his nose. "Do you have to be so crass?"

Demarcus took a moment to really study his friend. Jokes aside – which was often a difficult situation where he was concerned – Quinn looked worn down. "I'll mix you a drink."

"I don't want to get drunk," Quinn warned. "A beer is fine."

"One drink does not a drunk make," Demarcus countered, pouring a few ingredients into his martini shaker before replacing the lid and giving it several vigorous bounces. He poured the drink into a glass, added a cherry and pink umbrella for color, and shoved the concoction in front of Quinn with little ceremony. "Drink."

Quinn scowled. "I don't drink things with umbrellas."

"Drink it or I'll make you wear it."

Quinn rolled his eyes as he moved the umbrella and

sipped. To his surprise, he found the drink tasty and settling. It did wonders on his nerves, sending a warm sensation throughout his chest. "What is this?"

"It's called a Pouty Security Stud."

Quinn narrowed his eyes to dangerous slits. "You ask a simple question and … ."

"It doesn't have a name," Demarcus said, his eyes twinkling. "I just created it when I saw your face. For some reason I was inspired."

"Well, it's good."

"I'm totally going to turn it into a thing, though," Demarcus added. "If you like it – which is high praise indeed – I think other people will like it, too."

"Probably. What are you going to call it?"

"I just told you."

Quinn sighed as he rubbed his forehead. "Yeah, I should've seen that coming."

Demarcus' grin was cheeky. "I'm going to call it a Salty Seaman and put your photograph on the wall to sell it. I figure I'll be rich inside of a month."

"That could be a worse name."

Demarcus opened his mouth, something snarky on the tip of his tongue. He changed course almost immediately when he recognized the exhaustion plaguing his friend. "Were things that bad in Michael's office? I thought for sure he would take your side. He can't force you to spend the night in that woman's room."

"You know about that?" Quinn rubbed the back of his neck and made a disgusted sound. "Of course you know about that. The only thing faster than the flowing alcohol on this ship is the gossip train."

"If you need help … ."

Quinn cut off the gregarious bartender with a wave of

his hand. "Michael barely made an effort to make me do it. He asked. I said no. It was done."

"So, what's the problem?"

"I volunteered to tell Daphne DuBois that I would be entertaining myself for the evening – yes, I realize that came out dirtier than I expected, but I'm too tired to come up with something more verbally appealing – and I was looking forward to it," Quinn explained. "She was holding court in front of her executive team members when I found her on deck."

"That executive team thing is weird, isn't it?" Demarcus questioned. "It's like a clique inside of a clique."

"Yes, it's like high school all over again," Quinn intoned. "Anyway, she was making a big show about saying I was going to stay in her room. I pulled her to the side so I wouldn't embarrass her in front of her friends. Somehow I sensed that would be worse.

"The second we were away from the audience she changed her tune and said she was joking," he continued. "She wasn't sincere in the least. She was, however, trying to manipulate me. I was firm and told her that no one would be staying in her room and I would post a guard outside if she was worried. She kind of pouted and whined but accepted it and stormed off."

"That doesn't sound so bad," Demarcus said. "What's the problem?"

"The problem is that I was barely away from her when her assistant approached me and warned that Daphne would make it her life's mission to destroy me for embarrassing her."

Demarcus stilled, a mixture of surprise and confusion washing over him. "That's Penny Parker, right? Tiny brunette with big eyes, mesmerizing breasts, and always looks as if she's about to cry?"

Quinn nodded. "That would be her. She wasn't shy and reserved at all when she approached me."

"Why do you think that is?"

"That's a very good question." Quinn ran his hand over his hair and rolled his neck from side to side. "I cannot figure out why that conversation bothered me so much – other than the obvious, of course – and yet I feel as if something is there."

"Let me ask you this: Do you think someone tried to kill Daphne DuBois last night?"

"That's also bugging the crap out of me," Quinn admitted. "Rowan and I were on the deck, only about three hundred feet away or so. Granted, we weren't on the same part of the deck, but we weren't overly far away either. I think there's a good chance Daphne was close enough that she could've seen us."

"And what were you doing?"

"Oh, well ... ." Quinn's cheeks colored. "We were ... um ... talking."

"Uh-huh." Demarcus didn't bother hiding his smile. "Discussing the weather, were you?"

"If you must know, we were talking about the fact that it's harder when someone goes missing – like Rowan's father did when she was a teenager – than when they die," Quinn corrected.

Demarcus had the grace to look abashed. "Oh, well ... ."

Quinn took pity on the man due to his obvious discomfort. "And then I made a move to kiss her and was right there when Daphne started screaming."

Demarcus visibly relaxed. "Do you think she saw you and screamed to interrupt the moment?"

"I don't know." Quinn had a hard time wrapping his

head around that scenario. "That woman doesn't know me at all, so why go to extremes?"

"That won't stop a determined person when she sees something she wants," Demarcus offered. "Daphne DuBois is an entitled person. She feels the world owes her something. That's obvious every single time you talk to her.

"I can see her watching you and trying to throw a wrench in your plans when she realized what you and Rowan were doing," he continued. "You said yourself that you didn't see anyone on the deck."

"No." The part of the story Quinn kept to himself was the bit revolving around the death omens. He would never betray Rowan's trust and reveal her big secret, but he couldn't help but dwell on the symbols. Daphne boasted the omen first and then it switched to Penny. Why? "That doesn't mean someone didn't run before we got to Daphne. We didn't see her until she made a noise either."

"You don't feel that's the case, though, do you?"

"I don't know what to believe," Quinn admitted. "It's a difficult situation ... very difficult. I feel as if something is off, that there's something out there I'm not seeing, but I have no idea what."

"You could put a security guy on Daphne regardless of what she wants," Demarcus pointed out. "She's not in control of where security goes."

"Yeah, I already handled that." Quinn finished off his drink and shook himself out of his reverie when he saw Rowan walk into the dining room. She was dressed in a simple floral skirt and tank top, her hair pulled back in a loose braid. She looked comfortable ... and breathtaking. "Here's my date."

"She looks cute." Demarcus winked. "I wonder who she dressed up for."

"She always looks cute, whether she dressed up or not." Quinn got to his feet, momentarily sobering. "Have you been keeping your ear to the ground where Daphne is concerned?"

Demarcus nodded. "She's not well liked. Everyone talks about her behind her back. A lot of people hate her. She is respected despite all of that, though. People want to be her even as they're hating on her."

"Yeah, that's what I figured." Quinn flashed a lazy grin as Rowan approached. "You look nice."

"Oh, well, it's just a simple skirt." Rowan fidgeted as she smoothed the cotton material. "I'm sorry I'm late. I took longer in the shower than I meant to do. It was a long day with that conference and I lost track of time."

"It's okay. Demarcus kept me company."

"And invented a new drink," Demarcus added, his lips curving. "You guys have a nice dinner. Oh, and if I hear any gossip, Quinn, you'll be the first to know."

"Thanks." Quinn pressed his hand to the small of Rowan's back as he guided her to a table at the edge of the room. He wanted more privacy than the dining room afforded, but he'd resigned himself to a public meal ... and then hopefully a private walk. He brushed a kiss against Rowan's cheek before taking a seat across from her. "How was your day?"

Rowan's smile was enigmatic. "Well, it started off great ... ."

"We can agree there."

"Then it turned bad when I had to spend three hours with the Cara G Cosmetics girls during what had to be the most boring demonstration ever."

"Yes, I'm sure you're an expert on mascara now."

"It wasn't even about pitching the products," Rowan explained. "It was about pitching themselves as a commodity rather than individuals."

Quinn pursed his lips as he leaned back in his chair. "Meaning?"

"I don't know how to explain it," Rowan admitted. "It felt like one of those investment seminars where salesmen try to scam people into buying timeshare condos or real estate secrets."

"Hmm." Quinn rubbed his chin. "I'll admit that I don't know much about makeup. Do you think that's normal?"

"I don't know a lot about makeup either, other than you buy it at the pharmacy," Rowan replied. "This felt off to me. I honestly didn't get much of a chance to absorb it because Daphne sat me down for a talk after the fact so I was more focused on that than the demonstration."

Quinn's spine stiffened. "What did she say to you?"

"Oh, well ... ." Rowan averted her gaze, embarrassed. "It's really not important."

"It's important to me," Quinn prodded. "I had an interesting afternoon where she's concerned, too."

"Why? What happened?"

"I want to hear what she did to you first."

"She didn't really do anything to me." Rowan had a hard time keeping the frustration from creeping into her voice. "She just wanted to ask if the ship was always so dangerous. I swear she made it sound as if she was going to sue the cruise line company."

"I wouldn't put it past her," Quinn said. "Penny Parker warned me that Daphne might try to cause me harm – professional not physical, mind you – because I embarrassed her this afternoon."

"How did you embarrass her?"

"We're not done talking about you yet," Quinn chided, wagging a finger. "What did she say to you?"

Rowan swallowed hard, resigned. "She asked me if we

were together. She … um … made me feel uncomfortable because she was talking about you as if you were something to own instead of someone to spend time with.

"What's really weird is that she didn't come right out and say that she was going after you," she continued. "She kind of made noise about you spending the night in her room. She said she was going to have a talk with the captain and make sure that you were with her tonight."

Rowan averted her gaze, mortified. "I didn't say anything. I kind of sat there like an idiot because I didn't know what to say."

"It's okay." Quinn reached across the table and gripped her hand, softly rubbing his thumb over her knuckles. "You haven't been on this ship very long and you're generally not rude. You probably didn't know what you were allowed to say."

"That's part of it," Rowan conceded. "The other part is that I'm not in high school. I have no inclination to pull another girl's hair … or call her names … or start rumors about her because we like the same boy."

"Even if that boy is me?" Quinn's eyes flickered with amusement.

"Even if." Rowan rubbed the side of her head, as if warding off a headache that was barreling down on her. "We're adults so this dating thing should be easier than it was when we were teenagers. Daphne DuBois is still living in a world where teenagers reign supreme. It's … baffling."

"That's an interesting way of looking at it," Quinn said, tightening his grip on her hand. "In fact … ." He didn't get a chance to finish because Daphne picked that moment to appear at the edge of the table, Penny Parker acting as her shadow as the younger woman worriedly let her gaze bounce between faces.

"Oh, well, I should've known," Daphne said, her voice

low. "Is this the reason you can't do your job and protect me, Mr. Davenport?"

Quinn refused to stoop to Daphne's level and make a scene. "Ms. DuBois, I'm off duty right now and on a date. If you have security questions or concerns, you can call the on-duty shift commander and talk things over with him. His name is Fredrick Hamblin."

Daphne ignored the admonishment and focused on Rowan. "So you lied to me this afternoon."

Rowan balked. "Lied? How did I lie?"

"Ignore her," Quinn ordered. "She's been drinking and she doesn't know what she's talking about."

"I know exactly what I'm talking about," Daphne spat, her annoyance evident. "Ms. Gray and I had a very long discussion this afternoon. I gave her the opportunity to stake her claim on you. She didn't. She said you weren't her boyfriend. Now look at you. Someone clearly changed their mind ... or lied to me from the start. I'm guessing this is the reason I was treated so rudely an hour ago."

Rowan opened her mouth to protest, but she snapped it shut when she saw the odd look on Quinn's face. "What?"

"You said I wasn't your boyfriend?"

Rowan's stomach rolled. "I ... we're too old to be having this conversation in public," she growled, mortified when she realized a few heads were turning in her direction. "This is a place of business."

"Oh, whatever." Daphne made a dismissive clucking sound in the back of her throat. "I'm still open for offers, Quinn. This one is clearly playing games and you should realize that before she really hurts you."

Quinn's expression was unreadable as he pulled back his hand and heaved out a sigh. "This night isn't going at all how I expected it to go."

Ten

"Quinn ... ."

Rowan felt as if she was caught in a maelstrom, things spinning out of control as she fought to keep the ship upright. She expected Daphne to continue being a pain – that's the way she rolled, after all – but Quinn's reaction was completely out of the blue.

"Oh, what? You didn't want me to tell him that he wasn't your boyfriend?" Daphne made an exaggerated face. "Sorry to ruin your night."

She didn't sound sorry at all. Even worse, she slurred her words here and there and Rowan realized she was well on her way to being falling-down drunk. "You didn't ruin my night," Rowan said, pushing herself to a standing position. "You're doing a great job of embarrassing yourself, though."

"I'm hardly embarrassed." Daphne waved off Rowan's insult as if it was nothing more than a pesky fly attacking her lunch. "You're the one who should be embarrassed. You hurt this poor boy's feelings, crushed his heart."

Daphne shifted closer to Quinn. "I can make you feel better if you want."

Quinn heaved out a sigh, frustration overwhelming him. The expression on Rowan's face was almost painful. He wasn't angry with her. He had no right to be. That didn't mean her easy dismissal of their relationship wasn't hurtful. He had no intention of discussing that in front of an audience, though.

"Okay, well ... ." Quinn shoved out his chair and stood, shaking his head as he tried to get a handle on things. "Rowan, I'm going to walk Ms. DuBois back to her room. She's clearly not fit for public interaction this evening."

Rowan opened her mouth to argue and then snapped it shut. "Okay. What about dinner?"

"I'll meet you on the deck in a little bit. We can eat up there."

"Meet her on deck?" Daphne dramatically rolled her eyes. "Are you kidding me?"

"No, I'm pretty far from a joking mood right now." Quinn deftly grabbed Daphne's elbow and pointed her toward the door. "Walk that way."

"You're not the boss of me." Daphne attempted to jerk back her arm, but she was so drunk she almost toppled over. "I'm here to eat dinner."

"I'll have a meal sent to your room so you can sober up," Quinn informed her. "It's within my purview to decide when guests are too drunk to be left to their own devices. You've definitely crossed that line."

"I'm not drunk!" Daphne spat the words, spraying Quinn's face with saliva. He disgustedly wiped his face but otherwise remained calm. "I'm eating with my executive team. You can't stop me."

"It's okay, Daphne," Penny offered, flapping her hands

in front of her waist as she hopped from one foot to the other. "We can have breakfast tomorrow morning to make up for tonight."

"I don't want to eat breakfast with you!" Daphne said the word "you" as if she swallowed a bug at the same time and was struggling to hold it together so she didn't vomit. "I'm in charge here. Me!" She thumped her chest for emphasis. "I don't have to do anything that this guy says."

"That's where you're wrong." Quinn shoved Daphne toward the door, his jaw set and grim. He spared a glance for Rowan as he moved past her, his eyes dark and emotive. "I'll meet you on the deck as soon as I can. Get us a private table if it's possible."

"I ... okay." Rowan nodded. "I'm sorry for all of this."

"You didn't do anything you need to apologize for." Quinn managed to muster a smile for her benefit, but it was weak. He growled as he fought Daphne's efforts to remain in the dining room, ultimately forcing her to march past a bevy of curious onlookers as she gritted out a litany of complaints.

"I'm sorry about this," Penny supplied once she was alone with Rowan. "She's never like this."

Rowan tilted her head to the side as she looked the young woman up and down. She hadn't been able to spend much time with her – despite her best efforts to the contrary – and she figured Quinn might be busy for an extended period of time so she gestured to his empty chair. "Why don't you sit for a minute."

Penny widened her eyes, surprised. "I thought you were leaving."

"I think Quinn is going to be a few minutes with Ms. DuBois. I have time."

"I ... well ... okay." Penny dutifully sat. She was clearly used to being ordered around and didn't have a lot of fight within her. That was one of the things Rowan wanted to talk about.

"How long have you worked for Ms. DuBois?"

"This is my third year," Penny answered. "I honestly want to apologize again. She never gets like this."

Rowan arched a dubious eyebrow. "I very much doubt that, so there's no reason to lie."

Penny balked. "I'm not lying. She's a great woman."

Rowan decided to take a direct approach, and it wasn't simply so she could maintain proper time management. "You know these women talk a lot when they're broken up into smaller groups, right?"

Penny swallowed hard. "I ... what do they say?"

"No one likes Ms. DuBois. In fact, I believe the word 'hate' is bandied about quite often. They respect her and want to be like her, but they don't enjoy her attitude or company."

"That's just jealousy," Penny sniffed. "Mrs. DuBois is a great woman. Great women inspire jealousy. She told me that on the day she hired me. I realized it was true pretty quickly."

"Yes, well, I think a lot of women use the word 'jealousy' to cover a myriad of sins," Rowan argued. "I don't really care. We see a new group of people on this ship every week. It is what it is. I'm worried about you, though."

"Me?" Penny was dumbfounded. "Why are you worried about me?"

"Because you're stuck in a very unsavory position. You work for a woman you clearly hate – and she's not overly fond of you either, quite frankly. She tries to keep you down because she wants you to elevate her. It's standard practice in offices with a lot of female workers. Men are overtly aggressive when it comes to competition. Women? Not so much."

"I don't believe that." Penny smoothed the front of her peasant blouse. "You don't know Daphne. From your perspective, well, I'm sure she's been a pain. She's not easy to get along with but that's only because she likes things a specific way. That's not necessarily a bad thing."

"It's not," Rowan conceded. "There are different ways to get your point across, though. Ms. DuBois always seems to choose the hardest way possible."

"You simply don't understand her."

"No, I guess I don't." Rowan pressed her lips together and studied Penny. The woman was loyal. There was no way she would speak ill about her boss, at least in front of someone she barely knew. "You need to be careful. If someone did attack your boss on the deck last night, they could still be out there."

Penny knit her eyebrows, the shift in the conversation clearly taking her by surprise. "Why would anyone want to hurt me?"

That was a good question, and Rowan didn't have an acceptable answer. "I'm not saying anyone wants to hurt you," she clarified. "I'm merely saying that you need to be careful because your boss believes someone wants to hurt her."

"Believes?" Penny was smart and put things together fairly quickly. "You're not sure if anyone really attacked her, are you?"

Rowan shrugged. "I'm not in charge of security. You'll have to take that up with Mr. Davenport."

"He seems to have his hands full."

"Yes, well, it's been a long day for him." Rowan's smile was rueful. "Just be careful and walk back to your room with a group of other guests. You'll be perfectly safe if you do that."

"Okay, well, thank you."

ROWAN'S earlier excitement about spending time with Quinn had lapsed into weariness by the time she hit the main deck. She picked a table at the tiki bar, ordered burgers and fries in to-go containers, and sipped a chocolate martini as she waited for Quinn to arrive. She hoped he wouldn't be caught up overly long with Daphne, but the woman was obviously a belligerent drunk so there was no way to tell.

The evening air was humid and Rowan played with the condensation ring from her glass as she waited, expectantly lifting her head when a shadow obliterated the moon. Instead of finding Quinn, though, another familiar face floated into view.

"I ... ." Rowan searched her memory so she could place the man's face. When she finally did, she was more confused than when she started. "You're the guy from the shop on the mainland, the guy who liked my dress when I was shopping and wanted to take us out for drinks."

"You have a good memory." The man beamed as he sat across from her without invitation, extending his hand. "I'm Jamie Dalton. It's nice to officially meet you."

"Rowan Gray." Rowan shook the proffered hand, unsettled. "You're on this cruise? I ... why?"

Jamie arched an eyebrow, the question catching him off guard. "Is there a reason I shouldn't be on this cruise?"

"It's mostly cosmetic saleswomen. Do you work for Cara G Cosmetics?"

"Not last time I checked." Jamie laughed dryly. "I'm just here with my old college roommate. We decided to go on a cruise because we thought it would be a good way to meet women."

He was cheeky – almost charming, in fact – and Rowan couldn't help but smile. "You picked the right cruise. This ship is full of women ... and they're all ready to party."

Jamie chuckled, genuinely amused. "That was an accident. We're not complaining, though. I didn't realize you worked for the Bounding Storm until we had drinks with Sally that night. I would've pressed you harder to join us had I known."

Rowan realized it had been days since she talked to her friend. She'd almost forgotten about the woman's "date" with the two strangers. She hadn't bothered to ask how things went, which made her feel guilty. "Oh, well, I still would've begged off. Still ... did you check in through normal means? I take photographs of all the new guests on check-in day and I think I would've remembered seeing you."

"Yes, well, we saw that line when we got our room assignments and weren't really interested in photographs," Jamie admitted. "I think that's a chick thing ... no offense."

That made sense. Rowan didn't blame them for forgoing photographs. She remembered the line from check-in and it was obscene thanks to the special Cara G Cosmetics display. "That's okay. I would've known you were here days ago if you had waited in line, though."

"If it's any consolation, now I wish I would've put up with the line," Jamie teased, his eyes twinkling. "Oh, look, your drink is empty. What are you having? I'll buy you another."

"Thank you but ... ." Rowan wasn't in the mood for another drink. If she added more alcohol to the mix she would pass out in ten minutes flat. She didn't get a chance to convey that, though, because Quinn picked that moment to find her on the deck. He didn't look happy when he realized she wasn't alone.

"Sorry to interrupt," he grumbled.

"You're not interrupting," Rowan offered hurriedly. "This is Jamie Dalton. I met him on the mainland the day I was shopping for my new dress for our date. He and his friend – I don't think I ever caught his name – are staying on the ship. They went out with Sally that night."

Rowan talked so fast she almost stumbled over her words, but she was keen to make sure Quinn was aware that nothing untoward was going on. For his part, the security head looked amused rather than annoyed.

"You don't have to explain yourself," Quinn supplied after a beat. "I'm sorry our dinner got screwed up, by the way. I had quite different plans for our night."

"How is Daphne?"

"Out. I made her drink a gallon of water and then told her to go to bed. She kept trying to get me to join her – I swear she has invisible arms that come out when she's feeling horny or something – but she passed out fairly quickly."

Rowan chuckled, amused. "That's okay. I talked to Penny a bit before coming up here. I actually ordered us burgers and fries in to-go containers because … well … I thought we could take them back to my room and eat there."

Quinn's eyes brightened at the suggestion as Jamie shifted uncomfortably in his chair. "That's the best offer I've had all day."

"And I can see I'm in the way here." Jamie flashed an apologetic smile as he got to his feet. "It was nice to see you again, Rowan Gray. I'll let you get back to your night."

"Have a good time," Rowan called to his back. "Be careful on your woman hunt. You might get more than you bargained for on this particular cruise."

"That's what I'm hoping for."

Quinn watched the man go for a moment before shifting his eyes to Rowan. "If you'd rather go with him ... ."

The corners of Rowan's mouth shifted down. "Are you really going to go there?"

Quinn tilted his head to the side, considering. "No," he answered after a beat. "I'm too tired to go there."

"That's why I got food to-go ... and here it comes."

Quinn accepted the two containers from the waitress and extended his hand to Rowan. "Let's get out of here before we're interrupted again."

"That sounds like a plan."

ROWAN AND QUINN inhaled their dinner, offering minor bouts of conversation as they sat at the small dinette table in Rowan's room. The meal was comfortable, but the specter of heavy conversation hung heavy and obliterated the ambiance.

Once he was finished, Quinn wiped the corners of his mouth and gave Rowan an unreadable look. "I know we need to talk about all of this – we didn't get to compare notes properly before Daphne showed up – but I don't suppose we could table the conversation until tomorrow morning, could we?"

Rowan was surprised by the suggestion. She was also secretly relieved. "I can live with that. I'm exhausted."

"Me, too." Quinn gathered the empty food containers and dumped them in the trash bin before stripping out of his shirt and shorts. Rowan widened her eyes as she watched him crawl into her bed.

"What are you doing?" The question came out shriller than Rowan expected.

"I'm sleeping," Quinn replied. "So are you." He patted the empty spot beside him. "I promise I'm too tired to make a move. I'll give you ample notice before that happens so there won't be any misunderstandings."

Despite the surreal situation, Rowan belted out a laugh. "That sounds fair." She hit the lights right away, only stripping out of her clothes and tugging on an oversized T-shirt when she was sure Quinn couldn't see anything. She rolled into the bed next to him, snuggling under the covers as he pressed his chest against her back and spooned up behind her. "Um ... goodnight."

Quinn kissed the tender spot behind her ear. "Goodnight. I promise we'll talk in the morning. I'm just ... so tired."

Rowan patted the hand resting at her waist. "I'm tired, too. I was a little worried we were going to have a fight, if you want to know the truth, but I'm glad we're not."

"Oh, I didn't say we weren't going to fight," Quinn whispered. "We're simply going to sleep first."

Rowan's heart rolled. "Oh."

Quinn chuckled. "I wouldn't worry. I'm doubtful it will be a big fight."

Rowan brightened. "Oh, well, in that case ... thank you for the flower and I'll see you in the morning."

Quinn was already well past the point of return and he barely registered Rowan's words. "Morning. See you in the morning."

And with that, they both slipped into dreamland.

Eleven

Quinn woke first, taking the opportunity to quietly study Rowan as she slept. Her face was peaceful, the weariness that threatened both of them the night before seemingly beaten back. He rested his head in the hollow between her head and shoulders and sighed, content to remain exactly how he was until she woke naturally.

"You sound as if your mind is working a million miles a minute," Rowan offered, her voice sleepy. "I can hear something grinding in there."

Quinn chuckled as he tugged her tighter against his chest. "I was trying to be quiet."

"You have a certain presence that is stronger than words." Rowan stretched as she shifted to face him. "You look better than you did, though."

"You, too."

"I was worried you might fall down because you were so exhausted."

"We didn't get a lot of sleep the night before last and it was a long day," Quinn noted. "I feel much better now."

"That's because we slept for ten hours." Rowan

checked the clock on her nightstand to confirm her suspicion. "Yup. Ten hours. I haven't gotten that much sleep since I was in college and we drank until four in the morning."

"I'm not sure I've gotten that much sleep since I was a teenager," Quinn admitted, gently running his fingers over Rowan's temple so he could move a stray hank of hair behind her ear. "I didn't go to college so I'm unfamiliar with college partying habits. I was a good boy."

Rowan snorted, amused. "I've heard stories about basic training, so don't run that on me. I interviewed quite a few national guardsmen in my day because the Selfridge Air National Guard Base was local."

"Well, we might've done a little partying during basic training," Quinn conceded, smirking. "Only on the weekends and after a long week of training, though."

"I guess that's fair." Rowan exhaled heavily as she traced her fingers lightly over Quinn's bare chest. "How are you feeling otherwise? I mean, how do you feel about Daphne now that you've been able to get some rest?"

Quinn narrowed his eyes, agitation returning. "Are you asking if I have feelings for her?"

"No," Rowan answered hurriedly, shaking her head. "I was wondering if you were worried about forcing her into her room last night. I get the feeling she's big on complaining. I don't want you to get in trouble because of it."

"Don't worry about that." Quinn absentmindedly waved off her concern. "I'm not in any danger of losing my job. Even if I were, I wouldn't have done anything differently. That woman was out of control last night."

"I wonder why."

Quinn shifted his head so he could search Rowan's face for answers to an unasked question. "I think she's the type of person who is always in control so when she falls off the rails she does it with tremendous force. It's always worrisome when you're dealing with someone that tightly wound."

"That's true." Rowan scratched her cheek as she ran the previous night's escapades through her head. "So ... um ... about what she said ... ."

"About you not thinking of me as if I'm your boyfriend?"

Rowan nodded. "That's not exactly what I said when she questioned me."

"Okay." Quinn thought they would have a few minutes together before they hit the heavy stuff but he was eager to get it out of the way so he dived headfirst into the conversation. "What did you say?"

"First off, you should know that she made a big show about the entire thing," Rowan supplied. "She wanted to intimidate me. She asked if we were together ... monogamous ... and I was going to answer that we were and then I wondered if that was my place. I didn't think that I should answer for you, so I told her she would have to ask you."

"Uh-huh." Quinn's face was unreadable as he absorbed the information. "How would you have responded if you weren't worried about overstepping your bounds?"

"I ... ." Rowan broke off, unsure how to answer. "I don't know. Guys don't like being crowded and that's not how I want you to feel. We haven't been dating very long – which was exactly what I told her – and the entire conversation made me uncomfortable because it's not the sort of thing I expected to have to deal with at this point in the dating cycle.

"I mean ... she's a grown woman," she continued. "Daphne DuBois runs a million-dollar company and she's in charge of hundreds of employees and sales representatives and she made me feel as if I was stuck in high school again. I didn't like the feeling."

"I guess that's fair," Quinn hedged. "You should know that I wasn't angry with you because you said that to her. I also wasn't agitated because you didn't answer in a specific way."

"That's good." Rowan was relieved. "I didn't know because you pulled away really fast and it was almost as if you wanted to get away from me."

"I did want to get away from you."

Rowan stiffened. "Oh."

"Not for the reasons you think, though," Quinn reassured her. "I was kind of … hurt." It was hard to grit out the word but Quinn managed to accomplish the task, averting his gaze out of embarrassment. "I didn't realize until you said I wasn't your boyfriend that I wanted to be your boyfriend."

Rowan pressed her lips together to keep from laughing at the hangdog expression on his face. "Ah, so we are back in high school after all. I didn't realize the Bounding Storm was a portal to the past as well as a way to earn money for the future."

"Very cute." Quinn poked her side. "I knew it was unreasonable to feel that way and yet I couldn't seem to stop myself. It got worse when I hit the tiki bar and found you with that guy."

"Jamie?"

"I don't want to know his name. He bugs me."

Rowan burst out laughing. "You didn't even talk to him."

"No, but I could tell by the way that he looked at you that he was interested," Quinn argued. "I think I'm going to have to get used to that, though. My girlfriend is hot and we live on a cruise ship, so people are naturally going to hit on her whenever I turn my back. It's the way of the world."

"Girlfriend?"

"You heard me." Quinn propped himself up on his elbow so he could stare down at Rowan's surprised face. "I didn't want to get involved with anyone. You know that. Now, not only has it happened, but I'm also enjoying it. I don't want to look back. I want to see where this goes and I have no interest in dating anyone else."

"Don't you want to send me one of those notes where I check a box if I want to be your girlfriend?" Rowan challenged. "You know, 'do you want to go out with me? Check yes or no.'"

Quinn barked out a laugh, genuinely amused. "I can write a note if that makes you feel better. That seems more elementary than high school, though."

"Yes, you're right." Rowan tapped her chin. "We need a cootie catcher if we're truly going to be in high school."

"What's a cootie catcher?"

"It's a girl thing. You wouldn't get it." She ran her fingers up and down his well-muscled arm. "Just for the record, I would check the 'yes' box if you wrote me a note."

"Good." Quinn dropped a soft kiss on her mouth, sinking into it and ratcheting up the heat a notch when he heard her sigh. After a few minutes, he reluctantly pulled back and studied the planes of her face. "I think that catches us up on the heavy conversations, right?"

Rowan nodded. "Oh, well, other than me thanking you again for leaving the rose in front of my door. I did it last night, but I think you were already out by the time I remembered my manners. It's a beautiful flower, though. For future reference, you could've attached the note to the flower and made it really official if you were feeling adventurous."

Instead of smiling, Quinn furrowed his brow. "What rose?"

"I ... that rose." Rowan swiveled and pointed to the flower on the nightstand. "I found it in front of my door and thought ... you didn't leave it for me?"

Quinn shook his head as he studied the bloom. "I'm kind of kicking myself because I didn't think of it – although I would never buy a pink one because I now hate that color thanks to the Cara G Cosmetics people – but it wasn't me. There wasn't a note?"

Rowan shook her head. "That's why I assumed it was from you."

"I'm sorry, Ro, but it wasn't me." Quinn pushed himself to a sitting position, scratching his chin as he mulled the situation. "Did anyone else have flowers in front of their doors?" When Rowan didn't immediately answer he turned his full attention to her. "Ro, did you hear me?"

Rowan snapped herself out of whatever reverie she fell into. "Oh, um, I didn't look around. I guess it's possible that they were put in front of everyone's door and I simply didn't notice. I was really tired when I came back here yesterday afternoon."

"Yeah, I can see that." Quinn cupped the back of her head. "I'll ask around about the flower. I'm sure it's not a big deal. Heck, maybe you have a secret admirer on the staff, for all we know. He's going to have to get in line because I've already staked my claim."

Rowan snickered. "That's what boyfriends do."

Quinn matched her grin for grin. "You went some-where a second ago," he said, lowering his voice. "Where?"

"I didn't ... ."

"You did. Where? I would really like to know."

"You called me Ro," Rowan admitted, sheepish. "That's what my father used to call me."

"Oh, well, I'm sorry." Quinn wasn't sure if that was a good or bad thing, but he suddenly felt uncomfortable. "I can call you something else."

"No, it's fine," Rowan offered hurriedly. "No one has called me that in a very long time. It was … nice. That's all I was thinking."

"Okay, well, I can keep calling you that." Quinn drew her close and pressed a kiss to her mouth. "I'm sorry I wasn't the one to buy you the flower. I'll try to remember to do it myself at a future date. It can't be now, though, because then it would seem like I'm copying someone and I'm an original."

Rowan giggled. "You're definitely an original."

"You're an original, too," Quinn pointed out. "That's why we fit."

Rowan joined her hand with Quinn's and stared at the interweaving pattern their fingers made. "We definitely fit. Speaking of fitting, though, I don't suppose we could get some breakfast, could we? I'm starving."

At the mention of food, Quinn's stomach growled. "You and me both, Ro. Let's get ready for the day and hit the buffet, shall we? I could use a nice omelet and bacon."

"You read my mind."

Quinn smiled. "Not yet, but I hope to get there one day." He planted a firm kiss on her lips before rolling out of bed. "You have twenty minutes to shower and get ready. Now that you've mentioned food, it's all I can think about."

"UGH! **WHY** did you let me eat so much?"

Quinn was feeling pretty good about himself – the

heavy conversation with Rowan erasing any worries and doubts that plagued him from the night before – and when he pushed back his empty plate he realized he'd stuffed himself to what should've been unnatural limits.

"This is what happens when we eat in the main dining room," Rowan pointed out, finishing off her tomato juice with a flourish. "We stuff ourselves silly and then blame each other because our pants cut off circulation."

"What do you suggest we do about this?"

"We could eat in the employee dining room," Rowan suggested. "The food isn't nearly as good there and we wouldn't eat half as much. It would be good for our cholesterol levels at the very least."

Quinn made a disgusted face. "Yeah, I'm going to stick with the homemade omelets. I occasionally have dreams about them."

"You're a weird man."

"I occasionally have dreams about you, too."

Rowan blinked rapidly as her cheeks flushed with color. "Oh, um … ."

"You're adorable." Quinn shook his head, amused. "I wonder if I could combine those dreams. I mean … if I put you together with the omelet, I think I might be a happy man forever."

"Okay, that took a weird turn." Rowan wrinkled her nose. "Now I'm going to be plagued by visions of myself rolling around in a huge omelet … or wearing an omelet as a hat. Thanks."

"Don't mention it." Quinn's grin was lazy as he ran his fingers over Rowan's knee. Instead of sitting across from her he opted to take the chair to her right so he could touch her whenever he wanted. He didn't care if that they drew the occasional curious stare. He only cared about what he was feeling. It was a nice change of pace.

"There you are." Demarcus, his chest heaving, hurried to the edge of the table. "I've been looking everywhere for you."

"Define everywhere," Quinn ordered, working overtime to keep his temper in check. "We're having breakfast, by the way. I'll be on the clock in twenty minutes. Can this wait until then?"

"Uh, no. It can't wait until then." Demarcus vehemently shook his head. "As for where I looked, I started at your room and ended my journey at Rowan's room. They were both empty."

"So you hardly looked everywhere."

Rowan smiled as Quinn winked at her. "You found him now," she said. "What's going on? You seem worked up."

Now that he had a chance to better study the affable bartender up close, Quinn couldn't help but agree. "Is something wrong?"

"Oh, yeah. Something is definitely wrong." Demarcus lowered his voice to a conspiratorial whisper. "The maids found a dead body on the fifth floor."

Quinn's eyebrows flew up his forehead. "Excuse me?"

"You heard me," Demarcus gritted out. He was determined to make sure none of the guests overheard the conversation. "There's a dead woman on the fifth floor ... and when you hear who it is, you're not going to be happy."

"Penny Parker?" Rowan immediately asked, her heart rolling. She'd failed the woman despite the offered warning the night before. She couldn't help but feel guilty.

Demarcus shot her an odd look. "No, but you're close."

"Daphne DuBois," Quinn deduced, dumbfounded. "I ... are you sure?"

"We're definitely sure," Demarcus said. "We called

Michael to the scene and he ordered us to find you. He's not happy."

"No, I'm guessing not." Quinn exchanged a quick look with Rowan. "This is not going to be good."

Rowan couldn't help but think that was probably a grotesque understatement. "We should go there now. We can't afford to wait on this in case ... well, in case it's only the beginning."

Quinn understood what she was saying without further probing. He extended his hand and inclined his chin toward the door. "Come on. Things are about to get bad."

Twelve

Rowan fought her nerves as she followed Quinn to Daphne's room. He gripped her hand tightly until they got off the elevator, giving it a solid squeeze before releasing as he caught Michael's gaze. The captain, who was usually gregarious, looked grave.

"Is she really dead?"

Michael nodded. "There's no mistaking what she is for anything other than dead."

Quinn nodded, briefly locking gazes with Rowan before sliding past the somber captain. His gaze immediately fell on the body. Daphne was face down on the bed, her legs bent at the knee and supporting some of her weight as she dipped over the side. Her flaxen hair was askew, something Quinn hadn't seen since she arrived, and it sat at an odd angle on top of her head.

"What the ... ?"

"It's a wig," Rowan supplied, causing him to jolt when he realized she'd entered the room with him. "I figured it was either a wig or a weave given how it didn't move even when attacked by a stiff breeze." She leaned closer, studying the seam along the back of Daphne's head. "It's sewn in."

"Is that important?" Quinn asked, unsure what she was getting at.

Rowan shrugged. "I think it means she wanted people to think that was her real hair. If she was doing it so she could change up her look on a regular basis she would've used the wigs with the rubber lip." She gestured with her hands to show him how the other type of hairpiece slipped on. "This looks like real hair, which means it cost a lot of money."

"I'm still not sure why that's important," Quinn hedged.

"Her real hair was dark." Rowan pointed to strands of hair poking out through the bottom wig seam. "I don't know that it's important, but she was clearly trying to hide the fact that she was a brunette."

"Why not just dye her hair?"

Rowan held her hands palms up. "I can't answer that without seeing her hair. Maybe there was something wrong with it, the texture or something. Or maybe something else was going on. I simply don't know."

"Okay." Quinn wet his lips. "You can stay in here, but I need you to be careful not to touch anything."

"Oh." It hadn't even occurred to Rowan that she shouldn't enter. "Do you want me to wait outside in the hallway? I'm more than willing to do that. I didn't think. I'm so sorry."

"You can stay," Quinn repeated. "I might want your expertise on some of this ... um ... woman stuff she has on the counter over there."

Rowan arched an eyebrow. "Woman stuff? Are we talking tampons or wombs?"

"Very funny." Quinn rolled his eyes until they landed

on Daphne's body. He dropped to his knees, peering closely at her neck region without using his fingers to shift her hair and steadfastly ignoring her frozen gaze. "We're going to need a full autopsy, but I'm pretty sure she was strangled."

"Do you have someone on the ship who can do an autopsy?" The idea seemed foreign to Rowan. "I mean … you need a professional to do that, right?"

"One of the ship doctors is a former medical examiner. He can do it. He was hired because he can do it, in fact. He's paid well for his expertise."

"Where is he?"

"That's a good question." Quinn shifted his eyes to Michael. "Where is Dr. Dorchester?"

"He's on his way," Michael replied. "He had a late night and we woke him up as soon as we made the discovery. He should be here in ten minutes or so."

"Okay." Quinn rolled his neck as he stood. "I'm going to need an evidence case. We also need to see if we can come up with workable prints."

Rowan balked. "Prints? This is technically a hotel room. Won't there be hundreds of sets of prints?"

"In theory," Quinn confirmed. "The maids are pretty good and we can eliminate most of the prints by running them through our computers. Those we can't eliminate will go through standard background checks."

"All of the guests are printed if we have international ports," Michael supplied. "We're lucky because this ship hits two of those this go around. There are other ships that only hit domestic ports and they don't have fingerprints on file. We're the opposite … at least this time."

"Oh, I never even thought about that." Rowan squared her shoulders. "What do you want me to do?"

"I want you to look around this room and see if you notice anything out of the ordinary," Quinn instructed. "Wait until my guys show up with the plastic gloves. Once they do, you can touch things. Before that happens, though, I'm going to need some photographs of the scene. I'll call one of my guys and see if they can track down a good camera."

Rowan pressed her lips together and lifted her eyebrows. "Shouldn't I do that?"

Quinn covered his embarrassment with a cough. "I ... um ... of course you should do it. I forgot what you did for a living there for a second."

"I'll go and get my camera. Do you need me to bring anything else back?"

Quinn shook his head. "Just yourself. Try to be as fast as possible. I don't want the body moved until we have photos of every inch of this cabin."

"I'm on it. I'll be back in five minutes."

ROWAN SLAPPED on a pair of rubber gloves after finishing with the photos, her gaze steady as it roamed Daphne's slim back. Quinn was deep in conversation with Dr. Dorchester when she returned, the two of them clearing out of the way to give her room to work. Thankfully her time as a photojournalist taught her to detach emotionally from situations like this. Otherwise the body might unnerve her.

Quinn sidled closer to Rowan once he was sure she'd completed her task, erasing the distance between them so he could whisper. "You don't have to stay here. You've done more than enough."

"I have to stay," Rowan countered. "This is my fault."

Quinn stilled. "How can you say that? This is not your fault."

Rowan risked a worried glance at Michael but thankfully he was busy staring down the hallway. She couldn't very well mention the hopping death omen in front of him, but she couldn't forget it either. "I should've paid better attention to Daphne. I just assumed that she was safe."

"Why wouldn't you assume that?"

"Because I know how fast things can change. If anyone knows that, it's me. I let my dislike of her ... my jealousy ... get the better of me."

"That is not true." Quinn's tone was grim. "We can't really talk about this right now, but I promise you we're going to talk about it later. Until then ... stop blaming yourself."

Rowan pressed her lips together, forming a thin line. "It's okay. I can't go back in time to change it. All we can do is try to figure out who did this."

"We're still going to talk about it." Quinn pressed a quick kiss to her cheek. "Look through her belongings and see if you can figure out if anything is missing. I have no idea what we're looking for so use your best judgment."

"Okay."

Quinn was worried, but he let Rowan walk into the bathroom. He nodded toward Dorchester to give him clearance to begin processing evidence on the body. "See if you can get fingerprints from around the neck area. I'm pretty sure she was strangled."

"Let me see." Dorchester shuffled forward, his wire-rimmed glasses perched low on his nose as he knelt. "Yeah, I think you're definitely right. The skin is discolored and I'm going to bet that when I get in there her windpipe is swollen, perhaps even crushed."

"Can you give me an idea for time of death?"

Dorchester lifted Daphne's hand and narrowed his eyes as he studied her fingernails. "I don't see any skin under here so it doesn't look like she got a piece of her attacker. As for time of death, I need to get a better look, but given lividity I'm going to tentatively put time of death around seven hours ago so ... let's say two in the morning."

Quinn nodded, running the math through his head. "That was seven hours after I walked her back to her room."

"Speaking of that, you have an alibi, right?" Michael's expression was plaintive. "Please tell me you have an alibi, because if you don't, I'm going to have to put someone else on this and that's the last thing I want."

"I was with Rowan."

"Doing?"

"Sleeping."

Michael shifted his gaze to the bathroom but Rowan didn't poke her head out to engage in the conversation. "She'll confirm that, right?"

Quinn sighed, tugging on his limited patience. "We went to bed early because we were exhausted. We slept in the same bed. She'll confirm it."

"Good." Michael was genuinely relieved. "For personal reference, were you guys naked?"

Quinn scowled. "Do you always have to take it to that place?"

Michael shrugged, unbothered by his friend's accusatory tone. "I simply want to know if *you* took it to that place."

"Mind your own business." Quinn turned his attention to the cabin door, hunkering down so he could stare at the latching mechanism. "It doesn't look like there was forced entry. We need to check and see if anyone used the keycard entry after Daphne was deposited here."

"Did she have her keycard when you brought her back?"

Quinn searched his memory. "Yeah. She had to fumble in her pocket for it and she kept throwing herself at me while she was searching, but she had her keycard. I walked her inside, filled a glass full of water and put it next to the bed, and then left. She had the card in her hand last time I saw it."

"It's still here," Dorchester offered, gesturing toward the side of the mattress. "It's tangled in the sheets on the right side of the bed."

"She's still dressed," Quinn pointed out. "That means it wasn't a sexual assault, which is good for everyone concerned. She fell on the bed before I left, offered me a lewd suggestion, and then started talking to herself. I could tell she was going to pass out – and soon – so I wasn't worried about her wandering around the ship."

"She obviously got up at some point," Dorchester noted. "She's not under the covers and she either let someone in the room or woke up to find someone inside her room and was attacked at that point."

"It could be either situation." Quinn rubbed the back of his neck as he shifted from one foot to the other. "I'll check on the keycard reader. I'll send my men out to canvas the guests in this area to see if they saw something. So late at night, though, the odds of having a witness probably aren't great."

"That's one way to look at it," Dorchester supplied. "The other way to look at it is that if someone was in the hallway during those hours, the guests are more likely to remember."

"Unless they were drunk, which is probably a given since it was so late."

"There is that." Dorchester heaved out a sigh. "Either way, she didn't put up much of a fight. The alcohol could've incapacitated her, but the surprise of the attack might've put her at a distinct disadvantage, too."

"Or it could've been a combination of both."

"I don't envy you your job," Dorchester said, mustering a rueful smile. "I deal with facts. You have to put the facts together. It can't be easy."

"No, it's definitely not easy," Quinn said. "Keep me updated. It's going to be a full day."

QUINN WALKED Rowan to her office so she could upload the body photos to a flash drive. She was largely quiet for the trek and Quinn wanted nothing more than to comfort her. He managed to keep his hands to himself until they were safely inside, then he grabbed her arm and jerked her to him.

"This is not your fault," he growled, stroking the back of her head. "Stop thinking that."

Rowan widened her eyes. "How did you know I was thinking that?"

"Because I'm not an idiot," he replied. "I've watched you struggle for three straight hours and it's driving me crazy. Let it go."

"Let it go?" Rowan pulled back slightly. "Can you let it go? You were probably the last person to see her before her killer made a move. I know that has to be bothering you."

"It *does* bother me," Quinn confirmed. "It bothers me a great deal. I'm not the type to blame myself unless I've earned it, though. I haven't earned it in this instance. We had no reason to believe something was going to happen to her."

"Except for the attack on the deck, an attack we both discarded because we didn't believe her."

Quinn stilled. He'd almost forgot about the purported attack. "You have a point." He ran his hands up and down Rowan's arms as he considered their predicament. "I still have trouble believing she was attacked that night. Where did the attacker come from?"

Rowan shrugged. "There's a stairwell about thirty feet from that railing. Maybe whoever it was ran in that direction."

"Except Daphne said that it was a woman ... and that she practically disappeared into thin air and she couldn't identify which way the attacker ran."

"I forgot that she said it was a woman." Rowan knit her eyebrows together. "Could a woman strangle someone with her bare hands?"

"It doesn't take a lot of pressure to strangle someone," Quinn supplied. "It sometimes takes longer than you might expect, though, especially if you relieve the pressure long enough for the victim to get a few gasps of oxygen. Then you have to start all over again."

"That's ... lovely."

"It wouldn't have been pretty." Quinn rolled his neck until it cracked. "Given how Daphne was positioned on the bed, I think it was done from behind. That's the only scenario that makes sense to me."

Rowan arched an eyebrow. "So they wouldn't have to look her in the eye?"

"That would be my guess. Even if you hate someone, it's hard to watch a person die."

Rowan wanted to ask how many people Quinn had watched die, but she figured now wasn't the right time.

Heck, there might never be a right time. "So what do we do now?"

"Well, for starters, we're going to stop blaming ourselves," Quinn ordered, his voice firm. "You said it yourself, we can't go back in time and change things. We can only move forward and solve this, and we have a limited time to do it because the ship won't be on the open sea forever."

"You have a point. There's something else we have to do, too."

"What?"

"Take a new photo of Penny."

It took a moment for Quinn to grasp what Rowan was saying. "Oh. Do you think she's in danger? I assumed she was safe now that Daphne died."

"I've never dealt with jumping omens like this before," Rowan admitted. "There has to be a reason why. Whatever that reason is, Daphne was first on the chopping block and then Penny became the intended victim. Something happened last night to force the focus back to Daphne."

"And we need to figure out what it is." Quinn rubbed his chin. "We need to focus on what Penny did differently last night."

"And how are we going to do that?"

"We're going to run the evidence and then put together a plan of attack for questioning her," Quinn replied without hesitation. "She's probably going to be devastated by her boss's death, but that doesn't mean she's not a suspect. She had as much reason to hate Daphne as anybody."

"The problem is, I think any of these women could've harbored the hate to kill Daphne," Rowan noted. "Just because you're capable of hate, though, that doesn't mean you're capable of murder. Only one of those women managed to do that despite the rampant hate."

"So let's figure out which one it is," Quinn said. "The sooner we do, the sooner we can let this go and have another perfect date."

Rowan's smile was soft but earnest. "That sounds nice."

"It definitely does."

Thirteen

"What are you doing?"

Rowan jerked at the sound of Sally's voice, her finger inadvertently depressing on her camera button and capturing a rapid fifty frames on her memory disk. "You frightened me." Rowan worked overtime to calm her racing heart as she forced a smile for her friend's benefit. "Make a noise next time."

"Sorry." Sally smirked, completely unapologetic. "I'll buy a bell from the gift shop later and tie it around my neck."

"Make sure you pick a pretty ribbon."

"It won't be pink because, after this week, if I never see that color again it will be too soon." Sally made a face as she sat next to Rowan, wrinkling her nose as she watched her friend erase the errant photos. "Sorry about that. I didn't realize you were so worked up."

"I'm hardly worked up," Rowan corrected. "I'm simply having trouble concentrating." That wasn't entirely untrue. Rowan found it difficult to focus on the job she was hired to do when she really wanted to follow Penny from one end of the ship to the other so she could continuously snap photographs by way of protection. So far everything she'd snapped of the woman had come out omen free. Part of her was relieved. The other part believed something awful was yet to happen.

"Is that because Quinn so thoroughly rocked your world last night that you temporarily went blind?"

Rowan's mouth dropped open. *Was that really a thing?* "No."

"Well, that's disappointing." Sally made a sympathetic face. "I thought he would have mad skills in the bedroom. He has that look about him, after all. Is his technique bad or is he simply lacking staying power? We can fix both of those problems in time, by the way, so don't panic just yet."

"I can't believe I'm even having this conversation," Rowan muttered, shaking her head. "For the record, we haven't gotten that far yet. When we do, you'll be the first to know."

"But I thought he spent the night in your room."

"He did."

"And nothing?"

"We slept."

"Oh, geez." Sally vigorously rubbed her hand up and down her cheek. "Do you need me to rent some movies? We can probably find something when we hit port if you need inspiration. In fact, I think that gift shop on the corner by the lobby entrance has dirty books if you're desperate."

"No offense, Sally, but sex isn't my top priority right now." Rowan fought to keep her voice even so she wouldn't accidentally snap at the woman. "You heard we're dealing with a dead body, right?"

"I heard." Sally didn't look particularly perturbed by the revelation. "You guys spent the night together before that crone died, though. You can't really use her as an excuse."

"Actually, we can," Rowan countered. "She caused a scene last night and Quinn had to escort her to her room. By the time we got back to my room we were both exhausted. All we wanted to do was go to sleep."

"Is he a bad kisser?"

"No!"

"I don't understand this." Sally made furtive jerking motions with her head, as if she was a chicken and wanted to make her displeasure known to the rest of her flock. "I seriously don't understand this. Every woman on this ship has been salivating after Quinn since he arrived. We've built him up to mythical proportions.

"You got him," she continued. "You took everyone by surprise and grabbed him up, wrapped him in a bow, and tied him to your most precious gift in a way that seemed to indicate he had no escape."

"You have an absolutely filthy mind," Rowan complained.

"I was talking about your heart."

Rowan had the grace to look abashed. "Oh, well ... um ... sorry."

"I'm just kidding. I was talking about your lady bits." Sally didn't bother to hide her smile. "Are you guys waiting for a specific reason? I mean ... wait ... are you a virgin? Are you one of those beautiful unicorns who thinks she needs to wait until marriage? I've always wanted to meet one of those people. Have I finally done it and missed all the signs?"

Rowan heaved out a sigh and scowled. "I'm not a virgin. Why are you so fixated on sex? It can't be healthy."

"Because I want you to get some. I'm dying to live vicariously through your love life."

"Why not seek out your own love life?"

"I am." Sally grinned. "Focusing on yours is more fun than lamenting the lack of mine, though. It's just the way of the world."

"Speaking of that … ." Rowan was desperate to switch the conversation to a topic she could tolerate.

"Yes, I am a gifted lover." Sally's eyes sparkled as she smoothed the hem of her shorts. "If you're looking to secure a man for me, make sure he knows that fact out of the gate."

"That's not what I was going to say," Rowan groused. "I ran into one of those guys from the store the other day, though. I didn't realize he was one of our guests until he approached me. How did your meeting with them go? I never got a chance to ask."

"Oh, it went okay." Sally tossed her hair over her shoulder in a breezy manner. "They're nice enough, but they're completely full of themselves. I can only take so much conversation about a car – they're gearheads, which I find unbelievably annoying – before I want to punch somebody in the face. We had a decent enough time but falling for a guest is a big no-no."

"Because it's doomed from the start?" Rowan asked. "I mean you're dealing with a limited timeframe no matter what so that has to be difficult."

"The timeframe doesn't bother me as much as the fact that I hate people who like cruises."

Rowan stilled. "That doesn't make any sense. You work on a cruise ship."

"Yes, and if I didn't make a very good living doing it, I would totally pick another profession," Sally supplied. "I like the scenery, don't get me wrong, but cruise ships are annoying. You're still in the honeymoon phase when it comes to working on a ship. You'll figure out the very dark reality soon enough."

Rowan wasn't convinced that was true. "I kind of like it."

"That's because you have a hot man to cuddle up next to at night. Now, if he would just get up the guts to make a move. Do you want me to have Demarcus talk to him? Maybe we need to show him a movie, or perhaps get him one of those books. I can arrange both."

Rowan shook her head, resigned. There was no changing Sally. In truth, she wouldn't want to. "On that note ... I need to check in with Quinn. I'll catch up with you later."

QUINN WAS FOCUSED on his computer screen when Rowan walked into his office. He lifted his chin, a smile curling his lips.

"Hey. I was just thinking about you."

"You look unhappy," Rowan pointed out, resting her camera on his desk. "In case you're wondering, by the way, Penny's photos are clean. There's no omen in sight. That means she either escaped death because of something that happened last night or that's still to come in the next few days."

"Which one do you think it is?"

Rowan shrugged. "I have no idea. I'm not sure what to think."

"That makes two of us. For the record, though, I'm always happy to see you." Quinn offered a flirty wink before turning back to his computer. "As for me, I've uncovered a few interesting things."

"Like what?" Rowan couldn't stop herself from being

intrigued and she avidly peered at the screen over Quinn's shoulder as she perched on the corner of his desk.

"Well, for starters, someone used a key card to enter Daphne's room at a little after one in the morning," Quinn volunteered. "Time of death was set around two, but that's not official yet so we have some wiggle room."

"So you think whoever killed Daphne had access to one of her cards?"

"Not necessarily. Maybe Daphne woke up and left the room for a specific reason. Maybe she wanted ice ... or something from the vending machine ... or even confused herself enough to take a walk. She could've let herself back in the room and brought a guest with her when it happened."

"Do you think that's a possibility?"

"I think it is." Quinn bobbed his head. "If she let herself out of the room and came back in, she could've run into someone in the hallway. Perhaps it was a man and he wanted sex. He could've been equally drunk and tried to force himself on her.

"Maybe Daphne turned him down and he lost his temper and he strangled her from behind," he continued. "Then, after realizing what he did, he might've panicked and fled. He could very well not remember what he did, think it's a bad memory or something."

"I know that scenario fits the facts we have so far, but I don't believe that," Rowan argued. "Daphne said a woman approached her on the deck that night. She smelled perfume."

"What if it was cheap aftershave?"

"She runs a cosmetics company. She should know the difference."

"Yeah, even though I've worked hard putting together that scenario, I don't believe it either," Quinn conceded.

"That doesn't change the fact that she could've run into someone else in the hallway, perhaps it was one of her sales representatives."

"That's a possibility," Rowan agreed. "She was drunk so she could've said something ugly. Perhaps the woman she met was drunk, too. Things might've gotten out of control and ... strangle city."

It was a serious situation, but Quinn couldn't stop himself from grinning. "Strangle city?"

"You know what I mean."

"I do. That's not the only thing I found, though. We uncovered two sets of prints that we can't match."

Rowan pursed her lips. "Is that uncommon? Hundreds of people have been in that room. Has this ship always been used for international ports?"

"For the past five years."

"Oh, so all of the fingerprints should've been traceable. That's what you're saying, right?"

Quinn nodded. "Exactly. I ran both sets of prints through an external search system, meaning law enforcement avenues and a few other databases that I have access to through my contacts. I got hits on both."

Rowan widened her eyes. "Why didn't you lead with that?"

"Because they don't solve the case. They add more questions than answers to the equation."

"I don't know what that means."

"Do you remember our first date?" Quinn asked, leaning back in his chair.

"I'm pretty sure I won't be able to forget that night."

"Me either. When we were leaving, though, we saw all of those cops on the beach. Do you remember that? Well, it turns out they were there fishing a body out of the water. I did some checking after the fingerprints hit. The woman who died was named Jenny Lassiter. She was a Cara G Cosmetics representative and she was supposed to be on this ship but never checked in."

Rowan tilted her head to the side, considering. "Was she murdered?"

"She was strangled and dropped in the ocean," Quinn replied. "Fingerprints were discovered on her body, too. The same fingerprints we just collected off Daphne's body."

"Holy crap!" Rowan hopped to her feet. "How is that possible, though? That suggests a serial killer."

"Or at least a mission-based killer," Quinn clarified.

"Still, all of the guests were fingerprinted as part of the intake process," Rowan pressed. "Whoever killed Daphne should be on record unless ... well ... unless we're not dealing with a guest. That means it has to be an employee, right?"

Quinn didn't immediately answer the question. Instead he posed one of his own. "When you were hired, what was the first thing they did?"

"They made me take a drug test, asked me if I had any kinky sexual hang-ups that would make guests uncomfortable, and then they ... oh."

"Yeah, they fingerprinted you," Quinn finished. "All of the workers are fingerprinted no matter what job they're taking on. That includes maids and janitors."

"So how did someone who wasn't fingerprinted get on the ship?"

"That is the question of the day. I don't have an answer for you. That's hardly the most important thing I discovered, though."

"There's more?" Rowan couldn't help but be impressed. "What else did you find?"

"When I ran the second set of prints that didn't match

with anything in our database, I found they belonged to a Minnesota woman with a record sheet longer than Michael's tongue when he sees a woman in a bikini."

Rowan snorted at the visual. "Nice."

"I do my best."

"Who is this woman?"

"Her name is Claire Fisher. She was born in 1975 and has been arrested no less than twenty times."

"On what charges?"

"Drunk driving, theft, fraud. She's a grifter. She runs scams and tries to bilk old people out of money."

"And she's on this ship?" Rowan was understandably confused. "How did she get past the security protocol?"

"I have no idea. I do know that Claire Fisher was going under an assumed name on this ship, though."

"She was? Do you know her other name?"

Quinn nodded. "It's Daphne DuBois."

All of the oxygen she'd been holding inside her lungs leaked out as Rowan visibly deflated. "What? But ... how?"

"It's taken some time to put things together, but it seems that five years ago Claire Fisher fell off the map," Quinn volunteered. "She was arrested in Minnesota as part of some real estate scheme and she never showed up for her court date. She's technically a fugitive.

"Also five years ago, Daphne DuBois was a cosmetics dynamo who ran her business strictly on the internet," he continued. "She came out of nowhere and launched one of the most lucrative cosmetic companies in the world. It all stemmed from some line she ran for teenagers. One of those insipid Kardashian girls wore the lipstick and that was all she wrote. It was fame, fortune, and never-ending lipstick after that."

"So you're saying that Claire Fisher was leading a

double life," Rowan mused. "She was grifting while running this cosmetics company and somehow got lucky. What are the odds of that?"

"Not good. That's not what happened. At least, that's not what I think happened."

"I don't understand."

"Daphne DuBois wasn't a household name," Quinn explained. "She also wasn't a household face. No one knew what she looked like. She wouldn't do interviews and basically hid herself behind a website as she sold makeup by the bushel."

"So ... ." Rowan was having trouble grasping the bigger picture.

"So I think Claire Fisher tracked down Daphne DuBois, killed her, and took over her identity so she could run Cara G Cosmetics," Quinn supplied. "The real Daphne DuBois had no family that I can find, no one to report her missing. She had no husband or boyfriend. She had no children. She was a virtual recluse who just happened to know something about makeup."

"And you think Claire Fisher figured that out and killed her? But ... that's unbelievable."

"And yet it seems to fit the facts," Quinn offered. "You said the wig was sewn in. To me that indicates the Daphne we knew was in the middle of a very long con."

"So whoever killed her probably figured that out," Rowan mused. "Maybe it was even someone from Claire Fisher's past. What does that have to do with the dead woman in Florida, though?"

"That's what I'm trying to figure out. I've waded through a lot of this, but we still have more to go. I'm not sure how every piece fits the puzzle, but I'm confident I'll get there eventually."

"I'm confident, too." Rowan was lost in thought as she

settled back on the corner of Quinn's desk. "There's one other thing we have to factor in."

"What's that?"

"Penny Parker," Rowan answered without hesitation. "She was a potential victim at one time. We need to know why … and we need to figure out what changed to put Daphne back in a killer's sites."

"So we have a lot to do," Quinn prodded. "I guess I'd better get to it."

"We," Rowan automatically corrected. "We're going to get to it. You can't cut me out of this. I'm here until we figure everything out."

Quinn grabbed her hand and gave it a good squeeze. "Thank you. I'm not sure I could do it without you."

"I don't want you to have to try. Where do you want me to start?"

Fourteen

Quinn was calm when he ushered Penny into his office shortly after lunch. He was unsure how to proceed – giving Penny too much information could prove to be detrimental if she was the killer, but holding too much of it back would lessen the drama of the reveal. Quinn desperately wanted to know how Penny would take the information, and as Daphne's personal assistant, he could think of no one who was closer to the dead woman – or held the potential to know the secrets she held.

"Try to get comfortable," Quinn suggested when Penny caught her breath on a sob and rolled over into a fresh crying jag.

"How about some tea?" Rowan offered, taking a step forward. "I have a Keurig in my office, which is right around the corner, and some chamomile tea might make you feel better."

She initially wondered if it was wise for her to be present for the interview – she wasn't with the security team, after all – but Quinn insisted he wanted Rowan close. She had good instincts when it came to people and motives, and he wanted more than one set of ears on the interview.

"Tea sounds nice," Penny said, her eyes red-rimmed and glassy. "Thank you."

Rowan exchanged a quick look with Quinn before exiting the office. Quinn decided he might as well start with some softball questions to get the ball rolling. The key was to make Penny comfortable with him without tipping her off to exactly how big the stakes really were.

"I'm sorry for your loss," Quinn intoned, flashing a sympathetic smile as he sat in his desk chair. "This must've come as quite the shock to you."

"Oh, not really." Penny dabbed at her eyes, thankfully missing the incredulous look on Quinn's face.

"Not really?" Quinn wasn't quite sure what to make of the answer. "Why would you say that?"

"Because it's true." Penny mustered a watery smile when Rowan returned with her tea. "Thank you."

"Do you know something we don't know, Penny?" Quinn queried. He worked overtime to appear grave but not demanding. "We're trying to figure out who would have cause to kill your boss, but we're still floundering a bit this early in the investigation."

"I think the majority of the people on this ship wanted to kill Daphne," Penny admitted ruefully. "You see, I don't know if you've realized this yet, but Daphne wasn't a very nice person."

Quinn pressed his lips together to refrain from saying something stupid like "oh, we noticed" or "tell me something I don't know." Instead he rested his hands on the glossy desktop and flashed an encouraging look in Penny's direction. "Can you give me some examples?"

Penny nodded. "Well, take Andrea Gunderson," she suggested. "She's one of our one percenters – that's what we call the top one percent of sales women, by the way — and she's gotten a lot of attention since her arrival on the ship. Anyway, she was on the list, which means she earned a car in the next prize cycle, but Daphne said she wasn't going to allow Andrea to stay on the list because she felt Andrea cheated to get her numbers. She went to a beauty pageant and got half the women drunk before selling out her entire stock one day and it totally inflated her numbers. That's frowned upon."

"I see." Quinn fought the mad urge to laugh as he glanced at Rowan. She looked equally baffled. "Did Andrea threaten Daphne?"

Penny nodded. "She said she was going to yank out Daphne's fake hair and make her eat it. Daphne said she didn't have fake hair and to shove it, but Andrea insisted she would sue if she didn't get her car."

"And how did they leave things?" Rowan prodded.

"Angry."

"Uh-huh." Quinn rubbed his chin, his expression thoughtful. "Anyone else?"

"Everyone else," Penny replied without hesitation. "Sandy Petrelli said she wanted to kill Daphne for putting her in the blue sales group instead of the pink. She said Daphne was fudging the numbers and didn't want to reward her because she was fat and everyone knew Daphne didn't like fat sales representatives.

"Alexis Graham said she wanted to poke out Daphne's eyeballs and feed them to her because when Alexis' husband dropped her off at the ship, Daphne hit on him and offered him a spot in her cabin for the duration," she continued.

"Lauren Bishop said she was trying to figure out a way to trip Daphne when she was close to the railing because Daphne pulled her up in front of everyone at the conference and said she had 'man hands,'" she explained. "Lauren's hands are definitely manly, but she doesn't like having that pointed out.

"Oh, and there's this one," Penny added, jerking her thumb in Rowan's direction. "Daphne was laughing about going after her boyfriend – which I guess would be you. She said she was going to steal you from her and she couldn't wait to see if Rowan cried. She picked a fight with Rowan the other day and laughed when she upset her. She thought Rowan looked as if she was going to cry."

"Yes, well, Ms. Gray has been cleared," Quinn said, shooting a sympathetic look in Rowan's direction.

"By who?" Penny was legitimately curious as she glanced between faces.

"She was with me at the time of the murder," Quinn explained.

"You were in the same bed?" Penny seemed surprised. "Huh."

Rowan didn't know what to make of the reaction, but she was mildly insulted. "What is that supposed to mean?"

"Nothing," Penny answered hurriedly, recovering. "It doesn't mean anything. It's just ... Daphne said you two were just pretending to be together. She generally knew how to read people so I assumed she was right. I guess she was wrong this time, though, because you guys are really a couple, right?"

Quinn narrowed his eyes. Something felt off about Penny's reactions, but he couldn't put a name to what he was feeling. "We're definitely together," he said after a beat, changing course quickly as he picked a new direction to lead the interview. "How close were you to Ms. DuBois?"

Penny seemed taken aback by the question. "I ... well ... we communicated with each other every single day."

"That's not really what I asked."

"What did you ask?"

Rowan tilted her head to the side as she looked Penny Parker up and down. The woman was more than she appeared on initial glance. She knew how to play a room – and distract people when necessary. She also knew how to deflect. It probably worked well in cosmetic circles. She was in an entirely new arena now, though.

"How close were you with Ms. DuBois?" Quinn repeated.

"We communicated every single day." Penny looked almost smug when she parroted back the answer.

"Here, let me try," Rowan suggested, drawing Penny's gaze to her. "Did you ever talk to Ms. DuBois about things that didn't involve work?"

Penny perfunctorily bobbed her head. "Yes."

"What things? Oh, and be specific."

The light in Penny's eyes dimmed a bit, but she didn't crumble. "We talked about some of the other sales representatives – Daphne loved to gossip – and we talked about which colors washed people out. You, for example, should not wear orange, Ms. Gray. The color is too rich for your skin tone. It will make you look like a deranged pumpkin."

Rowan remained impassive while Quinn leaned forward.

"Don't talk to her that way," Quinn warned. "I know what you're doing and I don't like it. You might not think we have any jurisdiction because we're ship security rather than sworn police officers, but you'd be wrong. As far as you're concerned, we're the freaking FBI."

Penny swallowed hard at the words, shifting in her chair. She clearly thought Quinn was going to be a pushover and his response was somehow jarring. "I didn't mean to be insulting."

"That's exactly what you meant," Rowan countered. "It's fine, though. You learned it from Daphne. We made the mistake of believing you were under Daphne's thumb. You were using her as much as she was using you, though. It's good to know that tidbit moving forward."

Penny balked, surprised. "I ... that's not true."

"Oh, it's true." Quinn silently patted himself on the back for insisting on having Rowan present for the interview. "It doesn't matter, though. Nothing you can say is going to affect Ms. Gray because she's not insecure and you're used to preying on insecure individuals. Besides, she looks marvelous in orange."

Penny wrinkled her nose. "I wasn't trying to upset her."

"That's exactly what you were trying to do," Quinn argued. "It doesn't matter, though. Your petty glee at being mean is hardly the most important thing we're going to be dealing with today. Ms. Parker, I need your whereabouts for the early morning hours – let's say between ten and four in the morning."

Penny's mouth dropped open. "You can't seriously think I'm a suspect."

"I seriously think you've been acting odd since you entered this office," Quinn countered. "If you weren't a suspect before, you definitely are now. Where were you?"

"I was in my cabin."

"The entire time?"

"Well, no," Penny hedged. "I was in the main dining room with some of the representatives until about ten or so. Then we went to the tiki bar on the deck until about two in the morning. I went to my room after that."

"Okay, well, we're going to need names for confirmation," Quinn said, tapping on his computer keyboard before lifting his eyes again. "Oh, and just one more thing

... when did you become aware that you weren't dealing with the real Daphne DuBois?"

Quinn phrased the question in such a manner that everything hinged on Penny's response. He wasn't disappointed.

Penny widened her eyes to comical proportions and worked her jaw back and forth, flailing her hands at her sides as she feigned sliding in her chair. "What did you say?"

"Yeah, that was the worst piece of acting I've ever seen," Quinn muttered. "Be aware that we're confiscating your computer even as we speak – I'm sending a team to take it into evidence – and we will find out exactly what you knew and when. Lying isn't going to work in your favor."

"You can't do that." Penny narrowed her eyes to dangerous brown slits. "That's my property. You don't have the authority to confiscate my property."

"Read over the fine print on the document you signed when you checked into your room." Quinn adopted a lazy tone as he reclined in his chair, clasping his hands behind his head and shooting Penny a smug smile. "You basically told us we could do whatever we wanted, including acting as law enforcement representatives without warrants. You signed the paperwork so you can take it up with yourself if you're not happy."

"You can't do this." Penny's voice was low and dangerous.

"We've already done it," Quinn shot back. "Now, I'll ask again, when did you know that Claire Fisher took over Daphne DuBois' identity?"

"I ... ." Penny looked helpless as she glanced from face to face. "I don't know what you're talking about."

"Lying to us only makes you look more guilty."

"I'm not lying," Penny huffed. "I have no idea who Claire Fisher is. I'm telling the truth on that. I began to suspect that Daphne wasn't who she said she was almost a year ago. I couldn't prove it, though."

"Why didn't you call the police?" Rowan asked, genuinely curious. "If you knew she was a scam artist ... ."

"See, I didn't know she was a scam artist, although that does explain a few things," Penny admitted, rubbing the sweaty palms of her hands against her knees as she tried to calm herself. "I just knew that something wasn't right in the company. Daphne slipped a lot, admitted she didn't know anything about makeup a time or two. It was odd and I knew something was going on, although keeping track of all that stuff wasn't easy."

"Meaning?" Quinn prodded.

"Meaning that a lot of money seemed to be disappearing out of company accounts and when I asked her why she said to mind my own business," Penny replied. "I thought maybe the woman pretending to be Daphne DuBois was really an actress. There are a lot of rumors about the real Daphne DuBois ... and not all of them are pretty."

"What do you mean by that?" Rowan asked.

"We're a gossipy bunch," Penny explained. "A few years ago someone started the rumor that Daphne wasn't really Daphne and it caught on. It's like one of those urban legends you just can't shake."

"So who is she supposed to be?"

Penny held her hands palms up and shrugged. "I don't know. That's part of the game. People think she's an actress ... or maybe the sister of the real Daphne ... or maybe even a former criminal who is on the lam. Some rumors say the real Daphne is a man and he obviously can't be the public face of the company because people wouldn't trust him. Other people say the real Daphne was disfigured in an accident and she has no choice but to hire someone to be her public face because she would frighten customers otherwise."

"Uh-huh." Quinn was dumbfounded. He was fairly certain he'd never met a more shallow woman in his life – and he wasn't looking forward to questioning the other Cara G Cosmetics representatives if he could expect this reaction. "So you thought that the Daphne DuBois you were spending time with was an actress."

"Basically."

Quinn shifted his eyes to Rowan, something unsaid passing between them. "What if I told you there's a possibility that the real Daphne DuBois is dead ... and has been for almost five years?"

Penny gripped the arms of her chair tightly and leaned forward. "Are you serious?"

"Serious enough that I believe the future of Cara G Cosmetics is in doubt," Quinn replied. "I have to believe that whoever killed Daphne DuBois understood they were killing the company – and hundreds of successful careers in the process – when they did it. Why would someone go through with the murder if they knew that?"

"I ... ." Penny worked her jaw for a moment and then shook her head. "I can't think of any reason why anyone would want to do that."

"No, I can't either," Quinn agreed. "That doesn't mean that someone didn't do it."

"I don't know what you want me to say to that."

"I don't want you to say anything," Quinn supplied. "I want you to think long and hard about this, because whoever killed Daphne DuBois – or Claire Fisher, if you prefer – wanted to take down Cara G Cosmetics in the process. I don't think very many people wanted that. I need you to figure out who did."

Penny looked caught but she recovered quickly. "I'll definitely do that."

"Good."

Quinn remained seated until Penny left the office and then he hopped to his feet and shut the door before swiveling to face Rowan. "What do you think?"

"I think she's not the woman we thought she was and she's hiding a multitude of things."

"I think that, too."

"That doesn't necessarily mean she's a murderer," Rowan pointed out. "She could've been blackmailing Daphne because she knew she was a fraud. I don't think she'd kill her, though, because that means killing the company. You said it yourself."

"Yes, but I want Penny to say it to all of those women," Quinn said. "Penny won't be able to keep that little tidbit to herself. Before we know it, those women are going to be turning on each other because they're worried they're going to lose what they have."

"Is that a good thing?"

Quinn's smile was mischievous. "It is if we want them to start telling secrets on one another."

"You have a point." Rowan tapped her lip. "I suppose I should head up to the deck so I can listen when they start talking."

"You do that while I make a few calls," Quinn instructed. "I'll join you as soon as I can. We're finally getting somewhere. I don't want to lose momentum."

Fifteen

"You look lost in thought."

Quinn was supposed to meet Rowan on deck for a late lunch at the tiki bar. He couldn't stop smiling when he caught sight of her munching on a plate of fresh vegetables while she stared off into space, seemingly oblivious to the hustle and bustle around her. He thought she bore an adorable expression until it never moved, not so much as wavered … for a full five minutes. He stared the entire time and she never once shifted.

That's where Sally found him a few minutes later.

Quinn jerked his head in Sally's direction, recovering quickly when he realized he looked a bit demented staring at his new girlfriend as if she were on stage stripping rather than contemplating a murder in the middle of a cruise ship bar. "I was just … thinking."

"That's what 'lost in thought' means," Sally teased, shaking her head. "What's your deal? You're not considering doing something stupid, are you?"

Quinn arched a dubious eyebrow. He didn't spare a lot of time for the bulk of the ship's workers – mostly because he found gossip and nonstop partying insipid – but he was genuinely fond of Sally. "Define stupid?"

"Breaking up with her."

Quinn screwed his face up in what could only be described as a "what are you talking about" expression. "I'm sorry. Why do you think I'm going to break up with her? Not that it's any of your business, by the way, but I'm curious."

"You looked serious," Sally replied, the corners of her mouth tipping down to indicate she didn't find the idea of Quinn hurting Rowan funny in the least. "She doesn't deserve to be jerked around by you."

"How am I jerking her around?" Quinn was affronted. "Did she say I was jerking her around?"

"She hasn't said anything other than to stay out of her business," Sally clarified. "She seems to think you walk on water – which is kind of funny since we live on a cruise ship – but I'm a little worried."

"About what?"

Sally wasn't one to mince words and she didn't think now was the time to start. "The lack of sex."

Quinn's mouth dropped open. "What?" He sounded like a panicked high schooler caught doing something he wasn't supposed to be doing in the boys' locker room.

"You haven't had sex with her," Sally supplied. "Why? Is there something wrong with her? Before you get your panties in a twist, I asked the same questions of her. Everyone assumed you two were … you know. She said you just slept last night and nothing else. That's freaking crazy."

"Why is that crazy? We were tired." Quinn didn't appreciate being put on the defensive, but he could hardly ignore Sally's insight. He'd spent the past five minutes worried about Rowan's state of mind, after all. If Sally had information ... well ... he wanted her to share it with him.

"You're not gay, right?" Sally was fixated on the possibility.

"Not last time I checked."

"When was that? It was after high school, right? Most boys believe they're straight in high school because they want to be part of the 'in' crowd. If you're gay, it's okay. She needs to know now, though."

"Okay, I'm done with this conversation." Despite his curiosity, Quinn was fairly certain his ego couldn't take another hit from Sally. "Just for the record, I'm not gay. I didn't realize that taking a few days to get to know someone was such a sin. I'll keep it in mind for the future."

Sally's eyebrows flew up her forehead, his tone positively chilling her to the bone. "Wait a second." She grabbed his arm before he could stride away. "I didn't mean to hurt your feelings."

"You didn't hurt my feelings." Quinn was matter-of-fact. "I simply don't feel the need to go into this with you. I like Rowan. That hasn't changed. I know you're probably doing this because you feel protective of her, but it's really not necessary.

"We have our hands full right now," he continued. "We have a dead woman who was actually a grifter posing as another woman who may or may not be dead. We have hundreds of suspects because our victim was a horrible person. We have a lot going on.

"We just started dating and I don't feel the need to rush things," he said, rolling his neck. "I would much rather build a solid foundation before forcing the matter. If Rowan has a problem with that, she can talk to me about it. It really is none of your business."

Quinn's tone finally sank in and Sally looked sheepish.

"I'm sorry. I feel protective of her. She's different from the other types of people who want to work on a cruise ship, almost delicate because she's so sincere. You're different, too, which is one of the reasons I thought you would make a good match. I didn't mean to step on your toes."

"I want you to be loyal to Rowan because I think she needs it," Quinn said, choosing his words carefully. "There's a difference between being there for someone and taking over. You're trying to take over."

Sally's cheeks burned as she ran her tongue over her teeth. "You might have a point."

"Good. As for why I'm standing here, I couldn't stop staring," Quinn admitted. "She looks sad. Don't you think she looks sad?"

Sally shifted her eyes to Rowan, her stomach sinking when she realized Quinn was right. He honestly did have her best interests at heart. That much was obvious. "I'm sorry. I'm used to things moving a mile a minute on this ship. People never take the opportunity to relish anything, coast for a little bit. It's always full steam ahead. I forgot things could be another way."

"This ship skews people's perspectives," Quinn conceded. "I won't let it skew mine. I don't believe Rowan is the type of person who will let it skew her perspective either. She's strong."

"She's definitely strong." Sally bobbed her head. "I'm sorry about pushing her. I'll back off."

"That would be great considering what we're dealing with. I wasn't joking about things piling on. Speaking of that, you haven't seen any of these women act suspicious, have you?"

Sally tilted her head to the side, considering. "A lot of them have emotional and behavioral issues," she offered after a beat. "Some of that can be chalked up to the fact that they're homemakers and they go wild the second they can get away from their kids. As for being murderers, though, I don't see any of them having the potential for that."

"And yet someone here is a killer." Quinn heaved out a sigh as he scanned the immediate area. "This is a mess."

"You're preaching to the choir, honey."

Quinn mustered a legitimate smile. "Keep your nose to the ground and if you hear anything – even something small that you think might be insignificant but strikes you as weird – tell me. I need to start untangling this because we're running out of time."

"Plus we have port tomorrow," Sally reminded him. "If someone on this ship really is guilty, they might take advantage of a port stop and run."

"Yeah, I'm worried about that, too."

Quinn gave Sally's arm a squeeze before moving in Rowan's direction. Sally watched him go, conflicted.

"What's going on with the two of them?" Demarcus asked, inclining his head in the direction of the Bounding Storm's newest power couple, grinning as Quinn greeted Rowan with a short kiss. "They look all cute and cuddly together."

"I think I have a warped sense of relationships now," Sally admitted. "I just gave Quinn an earful about not making a move on Rowan and he pointed out they haven't been together very long. I just assumed there was something wrong when, in reality, he's doing everything right."

"He *is* doing everything right," Demarcus agreed, smiling when he heard Rowan break out in laughter. "They're kind of cute, huh?"

"They're ridiculously cute," Sally agreed. "It makes me sort of jealous."

"You and me both, honey. Still, I'm rooting for them. I

think someone on this ship deserves a happily ever after and I'm far too jaded to think it's going to be me."

Sally searched Demarcus' face with a prolonged gaze. "I don't know. I think there's still hope for you yet."

"Maybe there's hope for both of us."

"Maybe."

"AM I INTERRUPTING?"

Captain Michael Griffin gave Quinn and Rowan a saucy wink before grabbing the open chair next to Quinn and plopping his bulky frame in it. He didn't bother waiting for an answer.

Quinn managed to swallow his sigh even though he would've much preferred to carry out his lunch date privately. "Help yourself," he said dryly when Michael grabbed a carrot stick from Rowan's plate. "Don't ask or anything."

"Thanks." Michael ignored Quinn's tone and adopted a serious expression. "What do you have?"

"We have a ton of stuff," Quinn admitted, keeping his hand on top of Rowan's as he regarded his boss. "We're not sure how it all fits together yet." He launched into his tale, recounting the day. He left out anything that had to do with Rowan's ability and ultimately it wasn't difficult. When he was done, Michael was understandably dumbfounded.

"Are you serious?"

"Do I look like I'm about to climb into my clown shoes and do a little dance? I'm serious."

Michael snorted at Quinn's deadpan delivery. "That was nice."

"Thanks. I'm here all week."

"I don't even know what to say to that," Michael

admitted, dragging a restless hand through his hair. "Have you tried calling the Cara G Cosmetics corporate offices?"

Quinn nodded. "That's what I spent my late morning doing after talking to Penny Parker," he answered. "I wasn't sure how much to tell them so I asked for their lawyer to give me a call. I figured it would be smart to start with him."

"Probably so. What did he say?"

"He's calling me in an hour." Quinn checked the clock behind the bar to reassure himself he still had time. "I'm going to lay everything on the table. I need to know if he ever saw Daphne DuBois – the real Daphne DuBois – before and if he can describe the original version. I'm guessing he didn't ever meet her, though."

"What makes you say that?" Michael asked.

"Because I'm guessing that Claire Fisher slowly removed every old employee for that company when she took over," Quinn replied. "Think about it, she had to be nervous when it first happened. She couldn't suddenly be the public face of the company when the former one was a recluse. She had to take things slowly. She would never get another opportunity like this so she had to take over the company in the correct way from the start.

"So, she probably went in and replaced key personnel little by little," he continued. "If she'd done it all at once it would've raised suspicions and possibly caused lawsuits. I'm guessing she was smart enough to do it slowly and make sure she had cause when replacing people. That's how she survived in this position so long."

"But to do it she would've had to kill the original Daphne DuBois," Michael noted. "How did she get away with that?"

"I'm not sure yet," Quinn admitted. "I assumed she killed the original Daphne, but maybe I was wrong. Maybe

Penny is right and the original Daphne merely hides her face so she doesn't have to be in the public eye. Maybe she hired Daphne to impersonate her and she's not dead. The lawyer should hopefully be able to answer that question."

"It almost makes sense for the real Daphne to still be alive," Rowan mused, drawing two sets of eyes to her grim features. "The Daphne on this ship always struck me as someone who was living very close to the edge. Maybe that was a byproduct of having to live her life as someone else. Maybe she was starting to lose her mind because she couldn't differentiate herself from the newer persona."

"That seems like a legitimate possibility," Quinn conceded. "I don't think we'll have the answers we're looking for until I talk to the corporate attorney. In addition to that, I'm waiting to see what happens when Penny loosens her lips and tells the other representatives that the company might fold now that Daphne is dead."

"Is that true?" Michael was legitimately curious.

Quinn shrugged. "I guess that depends on whether or not there's a real Daphne DuBois. If the real Daphne and Claire Fisher were working together, that's one heck of a secret to keep for such a long period of time. If the real Daphne is dead, the company will be left floundering and I doubt it will survive."

"I've been watching the women while taking photos and I don't think the news has spread yet," Rowan offered. "When it happens, I'm expecting tears and meltdowns."

"You need to be careful," Quinn warned. "Don't wander off alone with any of these women. One of them might be a killer."

Rowan's face was blank as his words set in. "Why would they go after me?"

"Because they know you and I are going after one of them," Quinn answered without hesitation. "That could scare someone enough to make them act out in unfathomable ways. Speaking of that … ." He licked his lips as he locked gazes with Michael. "We need to skip the port stop tomorrow."

Michael was flabbergasted by the request. "Are you kidding me?"

"No, I'm not. I think that whoever did this might try to escape into a crowded port city. If that happens, someone may very well get away with murder."

"What am I supposed to tell the guests when they complain about skipping port?" Michael clearly wasn't happy with the suggestion. "They're going to go after me. You know I hate it when that happens."

"What's more important?" Quinn challenged. "What is corporate going to say if we lose a murderer? This story is going to be all over the news when it hits the mainland. Daphne DuBois – whether real or fake – is well known. The story is going to be all over the place. How is that going to look if we let a killer waltz away?"

"Yes, but we have one killer on this ship," Michael argued. "We have thousands of innocent passengers. They're not going to like being punished for something they didn't do."

"Then don't let them think it's a punishment," Quinn suggested. "Come up with a reason we can't stop at port … like a mechanical failure or something. You're good at thinking up lies, especially when it comes to women. Put your brain to the test now."

Michael wasn't convinced. "I don't know."

"I don't see where we have a choice, but it's ultimately up to you," Quinn said. "You can either be the hero or the schmuck. Take your pick."

"Oh, well, when you put it like that … you suck."

Michael crossed his arms over his chest as he pouted. "I hate being the captain sometimes."

"That's why they pay you the big bucks," Quinn said, grinning as he gripped Rowan's hand tighter. "I'm sure you can come up with something. You always manage to come through in a pinch and I'm expecting nothing less this time. We only have so much time to work with. We can't afford to make a mistake."

Sixteen

Rowan spent the rest of the afternoon taking photographs of the Cara G Cosmetics representatives. They were happy, for the most part, frolicking and having a good time with daiquiris and snacks. Rowan almost felt bad knowing things would shift for them, that their pleasant vacations would ultimately evaporate. If she wasn't so anxious she would've dreaded the switchover. Since things slipped from mundane to tedious at some point, though, she was relieved when the whispers began.

It started as furtive looks, a few women bending their heads together as news of Daphne's death spread. Rowan was impressed that Penny kept her mouth shut as long as she did. Within an hour of the news hitting a small group of big sellers, the gossip spread like wildfire. Before Rowan realized what was happening she was trapped in a sea of pink and the panic was palpable.

"What does this mean?"

Rowan did her best to remain small as she skirted the edge of the group and kept one ear on the conversation. Penny was suddenly the center of attention, the other sellers making a ring around her, and she appeared to be enjoying her moment in the spotlight.

"I'm not sure what it means, Madison," Penny admitted, lightly running her fingers over the side of the pool lounger as she reclined under the sun. Rowan couldn't help but notice that the woman had taken enough time out of her day to fix her hair and makeup before changing into a bikini so she could loiter around the pool. It didn't exactly look as if Penny was prostrate with grief when it came to her boss's demise. "I've got a call into corporate, but they're understandably reeling."

Rowan pursed her lips as she regarded the scene. It was a picture in organized chaos. The women whispered to each other in heated tones while also staring at Penny with a newly discovered reverence. Before Penny had been nothing but Daphne's put-upon assistant. Now she was the woman with answers, the only person in their midst who had any form of power. It was a startling transformation.

"What do you think corporate will say?" The woman Penny referred to as "Madison" seemed to be the designated point person when it came to asking questions.

"They seem to be just as confused as us," Penny offered. "They didn't find out Daphne was even dead until I called them. Apparently the security people on this ship aren't doing their job very well."

Rowan bristled under the statement but managed to keep her mouth shut. Penny was playing a part, she reminded herself. She wanted to get a reaction out of Rowan, nothing more. Rowan saw no point in giving the woman what she sought.

"How did she die?" This question came from a small redhead who stood to Madison's right side. She looked agitated rather than worried, which was an interesting shift compared to the other women.

"I'm not really sure," Penny admitted. "The security guy only said that she was found dead and he believed someone was in her room with her."

"How do we know it wasn't him?" A blonde in a purple bikini interjected. "Daphne wanted him from the first moment she saw him and we all know she was chasing him even though he didn't have any interest in her. Maybe he killed her because she wouldn't stop grabbing him."

"I considered that ... and even asked," Penny explained. "Apparently he has an airtight alibi. He was with the ship's photographer all night."

Rowan shifted from one foot to the other, uncomfortable, and tried to ignore the few curious stares that wafted in her direction. If Penny wanted to force her hand, make her stand up for Quinn, she was doing a good job. Rowan was very close to blowing her stack.

"Maybe they're in it together," another woman suggested. "Maybe the photographer killed Daphne because she was jealous and the security guy helped her cover it up."

"I guess that's a possibility." Penny smirked as her hardened gaze cut through the crowd and landed on Rowan. "She's right over there if you want to ask her."

Rowan swallowed hard when a multitude of eyes latched on to her expressive face. Instead of shrinking, which she was fairly certain Penny wanted, she squared her shoulders and fixed an affable look in place. She wanted to appear approachable if not outright friendly. "You can ask me whatever you want."

Penny's eyes narrowed slightly, but she didn't back down. "What did you and Mr. Davenport do last night?"

"We ate dinner and slept."

"And you're sure he didn't get up in the middle of the night to pay Daphne a visit?" Madison challenged.

"I'm sure." Rowan tilted her head to the side as she focused on Penny. "I couldn't help but notice that you left the most important part of our earlier discussion out of your retelling." Two could play this particular devious game and Rowan knew she had the upper hand. "Why didn't you tell them about the potential fraud and what that means for the future of Cara G Cosmetics?"

Penny's expression turned from innocent to murderous in the blink of an eye. "That's neither here nor there … ."

"What is she talking about?"

"Yeah, what is she talking about, Penny?" Madison challenged. "She seems pretty calm for a potential murderer and she clearly knows more than you do."

Penny wasn't thrilled with the way the woman stared at her and she flicked a piece of invisible lint from her shoulder as she made a clucking sound with her tongue. "They may have mentioned another issue, but I didn't think it was important enough to bring up now. We're in mourning, after all."

"I would rather decide for myself if it's important," the redhead said, taking a bold step in Rowan's direction. "My name is Sadie Markham. I'm the second best seller for Cara G Cosmetics. I would like to know what you know." She made the announcement as if it should mean something important, but Rowan couldn't be bothered to care about the hierarchy of sellers.

"Mr. Davenport found some interesting things when he processed the scene earlier this morning," Rowan supplied. "That includes a set of prints that, when tracked back to the mainland, lead to a grifter named Claire Fisher. That grifter also just so happens to be Daphne DuBois."

That did it. The new tidbit was enough to tip the women from potential panic to outright horror. They all started talking at once.

"How is that possible?"

"What does that mean for the company?"

"How did no one figure this out before?"

Rowan merely tilted her head to the side as she met Penny's accusatory gaze. She was practically daring the woman to diminish the importance of Daphne's real identity. She might try, Rowan realized, but it was too late to put that particular horse back in the barn.

"Everyone needs to calm down," Penny ordered, scorching Rowan with a dark look as she climbed to her feet. "There's no reason to panic. We have no idea what's going to happen yet. We should hope for the best until we know otherwise."

Apparently the other women felt differently because Penny was soon lost in a sea of angry pink petulance as the sales representatives gestured wildly and demanded answers. Rowan was relaxed when she took a seat at one of the bar tables and signaled the waitress for an iced tea.

The heavy lifting was done. Now she merely needed to watch the fallout.

"THANK YOU for getting in touch with me so quickly."

Quinn reclined in his desk chair and focused on the computer screen, giving the man who stared back a friendly smile. In truth, Quinn wasn't overly fond Skype and would've preferred a simple phone call. Preston Waters Dickerson III, however, wanted to talk face to face. Quinn didn't feel as if he had much of a choice if he expected the lawyer to work with him rather than against.

"It's not a problem," Dickerson said, tapping his fingers on his desk as he shook his head. "Is it true? Is Daphne DuBois dead?"

"She is," Quinn confirmed, bobbing his head. "She

was discovered by the maid service this morning. The medical examiner is finishing up her autopsy, but it's believed she was strangled at around two in the morning."

"Do you have any suspects?"

"Unfortunately we have an entire ship full of suspects … literally." Quinn licked his lips as he decided how to proceed. "Mr. Dickerson, I have some difficult questions. I understand you can't get into the nitty-gritty when it comes to the business operations of Cara G Cosmetics, but we've made some disturbing discoveries."

"Such as?"

"Such as the fact that we found a set of fingerprints in Ms. DuBois' room and they didn't match anything on our end. That shouldn't happen. When we ran them, we matched them to the name Claire Fisher. Does that name mean anything to you?"

Dickerson didn't so much as blink at the name, instead shaking his head as he swished his lips aback and forth. "Should it mean something to me?"

"Well, Claire Fisher was a grifter from Minnesota who basically fell off the map five years ago," Quinn explained. "She was wanted on an outstanding warrant and absconded before trial. Police have been looking for her ever since."

"And she's on your ship? Do you think she's the murderer?"

"No, sir, we don't believe she's a killer," Quinn replied. "We do believe, however, that she's our victim."

"I don't understand what you're saying," Dickerson hedged. "I thought Ms. DuBois was the victim."

"She is."

"But … ."

"Claire Fisher remade herself into Daphne DuBois," Quinn explained. It was obvious the attorney had no idea about the switch so Quinn needed to hurry things along. "We believe the transformation would've occurred about five years ago, although we don't have an exact date."

"But ... how is that possible?" Dickerson furrowed his brow as he mulled over the new information. "Daphne DuBois started the Cara G Cosmetics company almost seven years ago. That timeline doesn't match up."

"My understanding is that Ms. DuBois didn't make public appearances when she first started out."

"No, that's true, she was something of a homebody." Dickerson didn't grasp what Quinn was trying to say. "I'm not sure what that has to do with anything."

"Mr. Dickerson, I believe that Claire Fisher either struck a deal with the real Daphne DuBois to pose as the face of the company or that she killed her and took her place." Quinn opted to be blunt. "I'm not sure which theory I'm leaning toward, but both of them come with their own set of problems."

"But ... no ... I hardly see how ... that can't be right." Dickerson was flustered, his face flushing with color. "You're saying that the woman I've known for the past four years isn't really Daphne DuBois. That's what you're getting at, right?"

"I think that's the one thing I can say with any certainty," Quinn confirmed. "We know that someone started the company seven years ago. I do not believe it's the woman who died on this ship. I couldn't find any company sales or title transfer records, which leads me to believe they don't exist."

"They don't," Dickerson volunteered. "Cara G Cosmetics has been owned and operated by the same entity since its inception."

"And you started four years ago so that would've been after the time period when I believe the switch occurred,"

Quinn said. "So, my first question is, has anyone been with that company for more than five years? Is anyone there who can honestly say that the Daphne DuBois we found dead in her cabin this morning is the same Daphne DuBois who founded the company seven years ago?"

"I ... ." Dickerson worked his mouth, his mind clearly busy. Finally he shook his head and held his hands palms up. "No. I don't know anyone who has been with this company more than five years."

"That's what I feared." Quinn scratched his cheek as he rolled his neck until it cracked, the sound echoing through his quiet office. "We need to get in touch with local authorities in Missouri. That's where the real Daphne DuBois set up her company when she started, although I'm not sure if that's a real name or an alias adopted for business purposes."

"It's an alias," Dickerson offered. "The company was actually started by a woman named Danielle Studebaker. She was the sole proprietor and, yes, she lived in Missouri. I can contact the police and start moving on that."

"That will help," Quinn said. "I've talked the captain into skipping our port stop tomorrow. I'm worried that whoever killed Claire Fisher will try to run if she gets the chance."

"How can you be sure it's a woman?"

"Because I believe our killer had to know our victim and that pretty much rules out random guests on this ship," Quinn answered without hesitation. "All of the Cara G Cosmetics guests are female."

"I guess that makes sense. What's your theory? Do you think someone found out this Claire Fisher's real identity? If so, what is the motivation?"

"Perhaps someone was blackmailing her," Quinn suggested. "Maybe she was paying this individual off and something happened last night to shift the relationship. We do know that Ms. Fisher was unbelievably drunk earlier in the night. We're waiting for blood-alcohol levels to be tested and authenticated, but it's a safe assumption that the victim wasn't sober when she died."

"This is just ... I have no words." Dickerson shook his head, dumbfounded. "I'll call the Missouri police and see if I can find an address or phone number to track down Danielle Studebaker. It might take me some time. I assumed the Daphne DuBois I'd been dealing with was Danielle Studebaker."

"I understand that," Quinn said. "I'm not expecting miracles. I would, however, like a direction to move in if at all possible. If you can deal with the Missouri police I'll keep things in order here. We have two days to figure out who killed Claire Fisher ... and why they did it. That's not a lot of time."

"No, it's definitely not. What happens if you don't solve the case?"

"Then I have to hand it over to Florida authorities when we dock," Quinn replied. "I don't want to do that if I can help it. For now, we're watching the other Cara G Cosmetics women to see if we can find a killer. I'm not sure what else to do."

"Well, good luck."

"You, too."

"I think you're going to need it more than me," Dickerson offered. "I'll be in touch, though. This entire thing is a mess. The company may not survive this."

"I figured that part out on my own."

Seventeen

Rowan found herself instinctively snapping photographs as the Cara G Cosmetics representatives proceeded to melt down in fantastic fashion on the other side of the deck. She went through two glasses of iced tea while watching, steadily capturing images and internally smirking as she wondered what Daphne would say if she'd lived to see the photographs on sale in the purchase portal.

Then, because she realized it was maudlin to be thinking that way, she forced the idea out of her head and instead focused on the way the women interacted. She wasn't an investigator by any stretch of the imagination, but she considered herself a fairly good judge of character. From her perch next to the action – rather than in the middle of it – she realized she had a prime opportunity to see if any of the women were acting out of the ordinary.

"What are you doing?"

Sally appeared at the side of the table, a mixed drink in her hand. Rowan fought to maintain her composure even though she was seriously starting to wonder about Sally's catlike abilities.

"Seriously, do you ever make a noise?"

Sally snickered as she sat, grabbing a napkin from Rowan's stack so she could wipe the bottom of her glass. "I don't think it's that I walk overly quiet as much as you lose yourself in deep thoughts when you don't have anyone close to distract you and magically lose the ability to hear."

"I'm not lost in thought."

Sally arched a challenging eyebrow. "Honey, you're so lost in thought Quinn is going to have to leave bread-crumbs – or at least strip out of his shirt and flex – to get your attention and lead you back to sanity."

Rowan blew out a resigned sigh. "Fine. I'm a little lost in thought."

Sally offered her friend a reassuring pat on the wrist. "They say admitting you have a problem is the first step to overcoming it."

"Very cute." Rowan made a face as she sipped her iced tea. "I've been watching the Cara G Cosmetics women. It's turned in to something of a game, if I'm being honest, and I can't seem to tear away my attention."

"How so?"

"I'm trying to figure out which one of them is a murderer."

Sally widened her eyes as she shifted in her chair, studying the women. "Did they just find out that Daphne is dead? If so, I'm not seeing many tears."

"They just found out that the woman pretending to be Daphne DuBois is dead."

Sally made an exaggerated face. "Excuse me?"

"Oh, that's right, you probably don't know the entire sordid story yet." Rowan filled in Sally on the day's updates, and when she was done, the woman was understandably intrigued. "So ... that's where we're at. Quinn is in his office right now trying to talk to the attorney to see if he can get some answers."

"Oh, these women just got so much more interesting," Sally intoned, grinning. "I thought they were all empty-headed idiots. It turns out we have a potential killer in our midst. It's … fascinating."

Rowan made an exaggerated face that was obscene enough that Sally could do nothing but giggle. "You like soap operas, don't you?"

"Who doesn't like soap operas?"

Rowan shrugged. "My mother used to watch *General Hospital* religiously. It was always on when I came home from school. I got in the habit of watching it with her – even developing a really big crush on that guy who played Jason Morgan – but once she died I got out of the habit."

"That's kind of sad," Sally lamented. "I watched soap operas with my mother, too. I still watch them, though. It's one of the few things my mother and I can agree about when we talk on the phone."

"You're lucky to have your mother," Rowan pointed out. "I know she probably irritates you – my mother drove me crazy at times – but I would give anything to have her back."

"Yes, well, I don't know what to say to that because if I complain about my mother under these circumstances I'll look like a jerk," Sally admitted. "Talk to me about these women, though. Do you have a suspect you like?"

Rowan shrugged, noncommittal. "That's not really my job."

"Oh, you do like someone." Sally immediately warmed to the subject. "Who is it? Wait, let me guess." She surveyed the women for a long time, finally crossing her arms over her chest and offering Rowan a smug wink. "It's Penny Parker, isn't it?"

Rowan widened her eyes, dumbfounded. "How did you know that?"

"Because it makes the most sense," Sally replied. "I'll admit I did my best to stay far away from Daphne DuBois while she was on the ship – the woman could make a nun want to smack the crap out of her – but the few times I was in close proximity I heard her being extremely rude to her assistant."

"Really?" Now it was Rowan's turn to be intrigued. "What happened?"

"It wasn't anything major unless you're used to dealing with disgruntled underlings," Sally explained. "Most people wouldn't pick up on it, but I did. Daphne would endlessly pick on Penny's hair … or shoes … or the way her skirt fit. Penny would just nod and agree until Daphne's back was turned. Then, I swear, she would burn holes in the back of that woman's head with the hidden laser beams she had stored in her eye cavities the second Daphne turned in the other direction."

"Oh, well, that's pretty much what I witnessed, too." Rowan glanced back at Penny, who appeared to be having trouble reining in the boisterous women. "Do you think it's everything she thought it would be?"

"What?"

"Being the queen bee. Now that Daphne is gone, she's finally getting attention for something other than doing things wrong. I'm pretty sure that's how Daphne worked. She beat down those closest to her so she could always be on top. Now Penny is finally on top of a mountain that looks to be crumbling. She doesn't look happy, does she?"

Sally studied Penny for a very long time. "No, she definitely doesn't look happy. Speaking of people who don't look happy, though, check out who is watching her." Sally inclined her chin toward a spot near the starboard railing. "What do you think that's about?"

Rowan followed the woman's gaze with her eyes, shifting in her chair when she recognized the two men watching Penny with unveiled interest. "It's our two friends from the store. Have you seen much of them since we hit the ship?"

"Jamie and Gary? That's their names, by the way. Jamie is the one with dark hair and Gary is the blond. I've seen them to wave, but they seem much more interested in finding a new and different conquest each night."

"How do you know that?"

"They spend a lot of time in the main dining room," Sally answered. "I've never seen them working their magic on the same two girls twice."

"Does that bother you?"

Sally shook her head and then shrugged. "I think everyone wants to be desired, but those guys are too young and dumb to waste time worrying about their lack of sustained interest. In a week they'll be forgotten and I'll be dealing with two new over-sexualized morons."

It was a pointed statement and Rowan wanted to follow up on it further, but instead she picked up her camera and snapped two more photographs. "Well, you deserve better than them," she said, getting to her feet. "I promised I would check in with Quinn so I need to get going. I'll fill you in the second I have more gossip."

"You do that. I happen to love gossip."

QUINN WAS STUCK with nothing to do but wait for a call back from the attorney when Rowan came barreling into his office. At first he was excited – a nice round of kissing was sure to recharge his deduction skills, after all –

but the second he realized she was worked up for an entirely different reason his brain turned to business mode.

"What's going on?"

"We have a problem," Rowan replied, handing him her camera. "Look at that photo and tell me what you see."

Quinn was almost afraid to look at the back viewfinder, but he did as instructed, cringing when he saw the now-familiar symbol hovering over a strange woman's head. "Oh, crap. Who is that?"

"That is Madison Montgomery," Rowan replied. "She's the second highest seller for Cara G Cosmetics. Do you want to know how I know? She told me when I was stirring the pot on the deck a few hours ago. She made it seem like a big deal."

Quinn wasn't sure how to grapple with the information. "Okay, um, let's take this one step at a time. What do you mean you were stirring the pot?"

"Oh, well, I was up there watching the sales representatives like we talked about and Penny showed up," Rowan volunteered. "She's a real piece of work, by the way. I don't like her at all. I felt sorry for her when Daphne was alive, but now she bugs the crap out of me."

"You really need to learn how to form an opinion, Ro," Quinn teased, grabbing her hand before she could wave it about some more. "Take a deep breath and tell me what you're going on about."

"Penny showed up and told a few of the women about Daphne's death," Rowan supplied, sucking in a steady stream of oxygen as she attempted to control her breathing. "She pointed the finger at us – well, me in particular – and said her cohorts should question me if they really thought I was guilty."

"I'm still not following," Quinn hedged. "The women

thought you should be a suspect or Penny pointed the finger at you to make them believe you were a legitimate suspect?"

"The women suggested that I was jealous of your relationship with Daphne and perhaps I killed her and you covered it up for me."

"Well, we both know that's ridiculous. There's no reason to get worked up over that."

"I understand, but Penny told them to question me and she was so full of herself that I hardly recognized her," Rowan raged on. "She's just as bad as Daphne. It's as if the abused has now become the abuser. I don't like it at all."

"Yes, well, I like the way it has filled your face with color and how your chest is heaving. It's very … stimulating."

Rowan shot him a dour look. "Focus up here please." She gestured toward her eyes. "Anyway, the women started acting up so I turned the tables on Penny. I pointed out that she left out the part where Daphne was a fraud and the company might be in trouble."

Quinn couldn't hide his surprise. "Why did you do that?"

"You said you wanted those women melting down so you could gauge their reactions."

"I did but … ."

"I was simply helping along the situation," Rowan supplied, cutting him off. "It was actually a good thing because Penny didn't hold up well under the pressure. I'm sure she's going to complain about me – and probably you, too, because we're together – but I don't really care."

"I'm glad you don't care." Quinn was lost in the conversation, but he was having a very good time because Rowan was so animated. He couldn't ever remember seeing her so worked up. Of course, he'd only met her a few weeks before so she could be prone to dramatic fits for all he knew. He didn't think that was the case, but he was looking forward to finding out.

"Anyway, I dropped the bomb and left the women to freak out," Rowan said. "Penny tried to keep up with the questions, but then she kind of tuned out to what was going on. She seemed a little depressed. I kept snapping pictures, but then I got distracted by Sally and lost track of what was happening for a few minutes. Sorry about that, by the way."

Quinn stilled. "What did she say to you? If she bugged you about the sex again … ."

Rowan offered up a dismissive hand wave. "I'm used to the sex talk. That doesn't bother me. She'll calm down relatively fast. I'm sure of it. I think she's lonely and projects her feelings on us. That's the least of our worries."

"Oh, well, good." Quinn felt as if he was caught in a tornado. "Go back to Penny. I'm listening."

"There's not much else to say," Rowan admitted. "I talked to Sally a few minutes, we watched the guys who flirted with us at that store on the mainland check out the sales representatives, and then I snapped two photographs before leaving.

"I was in a good mood and planning to come down here and assault you with kisses when I happened to look at the two new photos in the elevator," she continued. "That's when I saw the symbol."

"And the symbol only happens when you take the photos, right?"

Rowan nodded. "It's not the camera. I've run numerous experiments. The camera doesn't matter. The only thing that causes the symbol to appear is me being behind the camera."

"Okay, I was just hoping for a bit of clarification." Quinn rubbed his chin as he slowly got to his feet. "I don't know what we can do. The Cara G Cosmetics lawyer is making some calls for me and we're trying to track down the original Daphne DuBois. I found out her real name and we're looking for her. I feel stuck until we find her ... or maybe even a body where she used to live.

"As for this Madison Montgomery woman, all we can do is watch her," he continued. "I'll make sure to have people in the hallway outside of her room tonight so we don't run into any problems there. We'll have a separate team watching whatever bar they decide to drown their sorrows at tonight. You and I can watch her in the dining room over dinner. I'm not sure what else we can do."

"I don't want to lose another one," Rowan admitted, chewing on her bottom lip. "I feel as if I fell down on the job where Daphne is concerned. I don't want that to happen twice."

"That was not your fault," Quinn chided, wagging a finger. "We've been over this. Sometimes things just happen."

"I don't want them to happen again."

"Me either." Quinn tugged Rowan to him so he could wrap his arms around her. "We can only do what we can do, though."

"I hope it will be enough."

Quinn brushed his lips against her forehead, swaying back and forth as he enjoyed the warmth of her lithe body. Then something she said earlier pushed to the forefront of his brain. "Did you said you were going to assault me with kisses?"

Rowan's smile was sheepish. "You heard that part, huh? Sometimes my mouth gets away from me."

"That's okay." Quinn beamed. "As long as it doesn't get away from me we're good."

"Does that mean you want me to kiss you?"

"Just for the record, Ro, you never need to ask me that question."

Quinn pressed his lips to Rowan's, cupping the back of her head as they both sank into the shared intimacy. They had a long way to go before they solved this one, but a small detour wouldn't hurt anyone. Er, well, Quinn hoped that was true.

Eighteen

Rowan changed her clothes before dinner, opting for simple shorts and a T-shirt rather than dressing up. As much she wanted to go all out for Quinn – and felt ridiculous for being such a girl given the circumstances – she figured it was better to be practical in case something dire happened.

Quinn met her in the lobby next to the restaurant's ornate double doors, flashing a smile when she rounded the corner. He held out his hand as she approached, inhaling deeply so he could get a whiff of her freshly applied body spray.

"What is that?"

"What?" Rowan looked around, confused.

"That scent. Your body spray. You don't wear perfume, but you do put on some sort of body spray. It smells like coconuts and it drives me crazy."

"Oh, that." Rowan's cheeks colored. "It's actually piña colada. I've always liked the smell. I figured since I was working on a cruise ship it was the perfect time to get it out and enjoy it."

"I like the smell, too." Quinn rubbed his nose against her cheek. "Seriously, you smell freaking good. You make me want to drink something with an umbrella in it."

Rowan tilted her head to the side. "That could be taken a myriad of different ways."

"As long as you take it in a good way, I don't care."

"Done." Rowan linked her fingers with Quinn and gestured toward the dining room. "Are you ready? I'm starving."

"I'm ready." Quinn led Rowan into the dining room, heading straight for the buffet line before scanning the expansive area. The seemingly endless sea of pink scattered over at least forty different tables didn't make his task remotely easy. "I don't suppose you see her, do you?"

"Look for the center of that pink ocean," Rowan instructed. "Madison Montgomery fancies herself important because of her sales numbers. The other representatives may not like her attitude, but there seems to be a pecking order they're required to follow."

"I will never understand women," Quinn muttered. "Oh, but there she is. You're good at this."

"Yes, I'm a master at many things," Rowan teased, grabbing a pair of tongs so she could pile as many crab legs as possible on her plate. "You should see me playing Candy Crush."

Quinn barked out a laugh, amused. "You're funny. I wasn't sure when I first met you. I knew you were feisty – and I definitely liked that – but you're funny, too. You don't take yourself too seriously. I like that in a woman."

Rowan pursed her lips, working overtime to ignore the heat creeping into her cheeks. "Um ... thank you."

"You also blush like a madwoman so I always know exactly what you're thinking," Quinn added, shaking his head when he saw her add scallops and shrimp to the mix.

"You might want to pace yourself on the seafood. We always have it and you seem addicted. I would hate to see you lose your love of crab legs."

"Oh, that will never happen," Rowan intoned, shoving three rolls on top of the crab legs and moving around the edge of the buffet table. "I grew up in Michigan. We didn't have a lot of really good seafood and it was always my favorite. Oh, well, I really love Middle Eastern food, too. You don't have a lot of that on the ship. I'm going to miss that. What was I saying again?"

Adoration bubbled up in Quinn's chest as he shook his head. "You talk a mile a minute when you're excited. I like that about you, too."

"Is there anything you don't like about me?"

Quinn tilted his head to the side, considering. "Not so far. Well, I didn't like it when you got embarrassed and said I wasn't your boyfriend. That's a pretty minor thing, though."

"Oh, well, I'll work on that."

"Good. Is there anything you don't like about me?"

Rowan immediately nodded, causing Quinn's heart to stutter.

"There is? What?"

"I don't like that every woman who lays eyes on you wants to hop into bed with you," Rowan replied. "That's a lot of competition for a simple girl from Detroit."

Quinn's anxiety faded almost instantly. "First off, you're not a simple girl. You're extremely complicated – but in a good way. As for the other thing, well, I can't help it if I'm a chick magnet. That's charisma. I was born with it and I can't shake it."

Rowan snickered, amused. "I'll keep that in mind. I would hate to blame you for something you can't control."

"You don't have to worry about that anyway, though,"

Quinn added. "My tastes run to simply complicated women from Detroit. All other women are invisible to me."

"Oh, that was a really good answer."

"That's a little gift of mine, too."

Quinn was still smiling when they found a table and settled, placing a communal bowl of butter sauce at the center to share and pressing their feet together once they were comfortable. It was a perfectly normal setting, except for the fact that they were spying on a woman who might be murdered thanks to a psychic symbol in a photograph. Quinn tried not to think too hard about that part of the equation because he worried it would give him a headache.

"So, did you do anything else today besides watch the Cara G Cosmetics women?" Quinn asked after a few minutes of quiet munching.

"No. How about you?"

"Sadly, I think we've shared every single thing we did today," Quinn noted. "I can't help but be a little disappointed."

"Yes, we've clearly run out of things to talk about."

"Except for books," Quinn interjected. "What's your favorite book?"

Rowan giggled as she cracked a crab leg shell. "Oh, well, I'm not sure I have one favorite book. I like a lot of different things. I'm a big fan of *Lord of the Rings*, Harry Potter, *Outlander*, Stephanie Plum and … well … I like a lot of different things. It all depends what I'm in the mood for."

"I like legal thrillers."

Rowan snorted. "I saw that coming. You're very law and order-y."

"You say that like it's a bad thing."

"It's definitely not a bad thing," Rowan countered.

"You have a very pragmatic mind, though. I'll bet you're good at math."

Quinn tugged on his lower lip as he considered the statement. "I am pretty good at math. How did you know that, though?"

"Because you like to solve things in a linear way," Rowan replied. "You don't really fall into daydreams or fantasies, which means you like real world applications when you're solving a puzzle."

"And that's different from you?"

Rowan shrugged. "I like a good daydream."

"Am I in any of these daydreams?"

"Only the naked ones."

"Oh, where is Sally when we're having this conversation?" Quinn lamented. "I would look so much better in her mind if she heard you say that."

Rowan wiped the corners of her mouth as she stared at him, her expression unreadable. "Are you worried about what Sally thinks?"

Quinn balked. "No. I just ... she's been a little intense lately."

"You can't let her get to you," Rowan chided. "I told you that she's lonely. That's where all of the questions and teasing stem from. She doesn't mean to be overbearing."

"Did she tell you that?" Quinn found, strangely enough, that his heart pinged with worry when Rowan mentioned Sally's potential loneliness. "She always seems as if she's the life of the party. I would hate to think of her being lonely."

"She doesn't realize she's lonely," Rowan supplied. "She thinks she's fine. We can't do anything for her until she realizes it."

"And how do you know that?" Quinn was fascinated with the way Rowan's mind worked.

"Because I see it … and I recognize it from my last year in Detroit," Rowan admitted, averting her gaze. "I thought I was upset when I lost my job. It took me two weeks to realize that wasn't the case. I wasn't upset about the job even though I was worried about paying my bills. I was upset because I was lonely.

"Even though I worked and lived in Detroit, I didn't have a lot of friends," she continued. "I had co-workers and was never at a loss for conversation, but intimacy is a different animal. Intimacy is one of those things that people crave whether they realize it or not."

Quinn rolled the idea through his head and found that he believed the statement to be true. "I didn't realize what I was missing until I started spending time with you."

"You're not talking about sex, right?" Rowan's tone was dry.

Quinn chuckled, legitimately amused. "No. I'm talking about this." He gestured toward the table. "I'm talking about this." He thumped his foot on top of hers. "Just the simple act of eating dinner with you, talking about books and our friend who is lonely, fills me up with something I didn't know I was lacking until you came along."

"Oh, that's almost poetic," Rowan teased, her eyes flashing. "This is nice, though." She ran her foot up and down Quinn's calf to anchor the point. "As for the rest, it will happen when it's supposed to happen. I'm a big believer in fate."

She was earnest but Quinn couldn't help but question the notion. "If you believe in fate, why are you beating yourself up for what happened to Daphne?"

"I … ." Rowan broke off, silently working her jaw as she decided how to answer. "That's a good point. I guess I have a lot of guilt that follows me around sometimes. I've never been able to shake it."

"Because you blame yourself when someone dies," Quinn mused. "You think you could've stopped it ... or saved them ... or changed the outcome. I know that's hard for you to deal with and I don't blame you for wondering, but you cannot carry the guilt of the world on your shoulders. They're not big enough to hold up that much weight."

"What you're saying makes sense in my head, but my heart always takes a while to catch up," Rowan admitted. "I don't blame myself for what happened to Daphne, and somehow knowing she was a fraud and might've done something dishonest eased my guilt when that probably shouldn't have been the case."

"I don't believe that," Quinn countered. "Daphne wasn't a good person. Heck, Daphne wasn't her real name. Claire Fisher was a disturbed woman who made it her life's goal to scam innocent people out of their hard-earned money before she fell into this gig.

"Now, we don't know what happened and we certainly don't know if the real Daphne DuBois is alive or dead," he continued. "That doesn't mean Claire Fisher was a good person, or absolve her of her sins if she was trying to redeem herself. She died, and that's terrible. I want someone to pay for murdering her. That doesn't mean I feel guilt over what happened."

"Because she kept hitting on you and wanted to grab your ... um ... coconut spray?"

Quinn's face split with a wide grin. "You're very witty. I love that about you."

"And we're back to the compliment festival," Rowan teased. "Do you know what I really like about you? You're good at making me feel better. I have a tendency to disappear into my own head when I'm feeling guilty. You haven't allowed me to do that once today."

"And I'm not going to let you do it tomorrow … or the next day … or next week, for that matter," Quinn said. "You have nothing to feel guilty about. You're doing the very best that you can. We'll take this one step at a time and go from there. That's all we can do."

"I know." Rowan flashed a rueful smile. "These crab legs are very good, by the way. I'm never going to get tired of them. I don't care what you say."

"We'll see." Quinn smirked as the duo fell into amiable silence. For a long time the only sound emanating from the table was cracking crustacean appendages.

After finishing off the bulk of her seafood, Rowan shifted her eyes back to Madison and jerked her head to the side when she realized the woman wasn't sitting alone. She also wasn't merely sitting with her Cara G Cosmetics brethren. No, she'd picked up a new friend.

"Huh."

"Huh, what?" Quinn asked, turning so he could see what had caught Rowan's attention. "Isn't that your friend from the other night?"

"I wouldn't call him my friend, but that's definitely the guy who was sitting with me," Rowan replied, her mind busy. "I think he said his name was Jamie Dalton. Sally talked about him this afternoon and said his friend was Gary something or other."

"Is that his confirmation name?"

Rowan snickered. "I don't know that I've ever caught his last name. I haven't really talked to him."

"What do you make of them?"

"I don't particularly like them," Rowan replied after a beat. "I thought they were flirty but harmless that day at the store. Since then, though, I'm not sure what to think."

Quinn forgot about his dinner and focused on Rowan's conflicted features. "Do you want to expound on that?"

"There's something about them I don't like ... and I definitely don't trust them," Rowan admitted. "They made a big deal of asking Sally and me out that day we met them in the store. I said I was busy, but Sally agreed to meet them at the tiki bar close to the ship. You know the one I'm talking about, right?"

Quinn nodded. "That was smart of her. That bar is always packed with Bounding Storm workers. She wouldn't have been in any trouble if they turned out to be dangerous because she would've had backup."

"I think that's why she picked it," Rowan admitted. "She was flirting with them and they were flirting with her, but she's cooled on them considerably since then. She didn't say much but admitted they flirted with everyone and never focused on the same woman two nights in a row."

"Well, not to stand up for them because they sound like jerks, I think that's fairly normal for guys that age who are on a cruise ship," Quinn offered. "I'm sure Sally didn't think she was going to get a happily ever after with either of those guys."

"I'm sure she didn't either," Rowan agreed. "She didn't seem fond of them, though, and when I talked to Jamie the other night he seemed a little intense. I don't know ... it's probably nothing, but I don't like them. They make me uncomfortable."

Quinn's expression was thoughtful as he focused on the two men. "They were on the beach the night that woman was fished from the ocean," he mused aloud. "That bar is closer to the spot where the body was recovered than where we were. That could be a coincidence but ... maybe they're worth looking into."

Rowan couldn't help but be surprised by the suggestion. "I thought we were looking for a woman."

"Yes, but what if we're focusing on a woman to the detriment of our own case. Just because Daphne insisted it was a woman who approached her on the deck that first night, that doesn't mean she was telling the truth. We can't base our investigation on what she said because we've since found out she lied for a living."

"That's true." Rowan wrinkled her nose. "Do you think it's possible?"

"There's only one way to find out." Quinn wiped his mouth with a napkin and turned backed to his dinner. "Let's finish up here and then go to my office. We can run the registrations and see what we come up with."

"That sounds like a plan."

"And then you can assault me with kisses again," Quinn added. "I enjoyed that a great deal."

"That sounds like a better plan."

Nineteen

"Anything?"

Quinn fought to contain his amusement as Rowan paced the same small strip of floor at the front of his office. She seemed agitated, ready for action, and altogether cute when she screwed up her face in concentration.

"You need to give me a chance to boot up the computer," Quinn said, smirking. "I haven't inputted their names yet."

"Oh, well, sorry." Rowan looked sheepish as she sat in one of the chairs across from his desk. "Now that you've suggested we look into Jamie and Gary I can't get the possibility of them being involved out of my head."

"Have you taken any photos of them?"

"I ... hmm." Rowan tilted her head to the side as she racked her brain. "That's a really good question and I don't think I have."

"Is that unusual? I thought you were supposed to take at least one photo of each guest during their stay."

"I am ... and I have. At least I've taken photos of everyone on the registry. I know I have. I double-checked today. I was antsy this afternoon watching the Cara G Cosmetics women and I went through my list a second time to make sure I'd covered my bases. I caught everyone on the registry list."

"But ... ." Quinn furrowed his brow as he typed in his password and waited for the computer to continue cycling through its startup routine. "Would you remember taking photographs of those guys?"

"I should think so. I've grown to dislike them so they would stand out in a sea of faces I don't recognize."

"So even if they were registered under different names you would've caught that," Quinn mused aloud. "What about when they checked in?"

Rowan immediately started shaking her head. "When Jamie approached me the other night at the tiki bar I was surprised. I had no idea he was on the ship. That in itself should've been curious, but I was so caught up with all of the Daphne stuff – and this was before we found her dead, mind you – that I didn't think much about it."

"Did you ask him about it?" Quinn had no idea why – perhaps it was because he loved a good mystery – but he was rapidly warming to the idea of taking a closer look at Jamie and Gary.

"I did." Rowan bobbed her head as she traced the contour of her bottom lip with her fingertip. "I mentioned that I didn't see him for check-in photos. I don't know if you remember taking a look at the lobby that day, but I had two backdrops. Even though the Cara G Cosmetics group was massive, they only accounted for a good twenty-five percent of the guests. The rest of the guests had a normal backdrop."

"I stopped in to see you that day, but you were already worked up," Quinn noted. "I didn't pay attention to the backdrops. Heck, I rarely pay attention to the backdrops. I believe you, though."

"I asked Jamie about it because I was searching for a way to make conversation while I waited for you," Rowan explained. "I was a little nervous – that was the night you got upset about the 'he's my boyfriend, he's not my boyfriend' thing and I thought you might pick a fight when you came back. Then, of course, I let my imagination get away from me and wondered if you planned on coming back at all."

Quinn's expression softened. "I was always coming back."

"Yeah, but I thought maybe Daphne would throw herself at you and ... ."

"I would stay with her?" Quinn arched a challenging eyebrow, his temper flaring.

Rowan shook her head. "I thought maybe she might get sick and you're a good guy so you would stay long enough to make sure she was okay. Then, rather than come to my room and risk a fight, I figured you might go to your own room. I worked out an entire scenario where you were too angry to even look at me."

Quinn snorted as he brought up the Bounding Storm's internal registry. "That's quite an imagination you've got there, Ro."

"I think it's from being an only child," she admitted ruefully. "I used to make up all kinds of things to entertain myself when I was a kid. I didn't have a lot of friends because my parents were afraid to let me wander around the neighborhood on my own. I had to come up with ways to entertain myself. That's why I read so much."

"Did you live in a dangerous neighborhood?"

"Not really."

"Then why didn't they want you hanging out with the other kids?"

"I ... um ... huh." Rowan knit her eyebrows together as she mulled the question. "I have no idea. I never really thought about it. They were extremely protective of me and I guess it seemed normal."

"Well, that doesn't sound normal to me," Quinn argued. "Most days my mother told me to leave the house before ten and not come back until dinner."

"You didn't grow up in Detroit."

"Fair enough, but it sounds like you didn't grow up in Detroit either," he said. "You grew up in a suburb, right?"

Rowan nodded, conflicted. "I don't know why they wanted to keep me so isolated. I never asked and now it's too late to find out the answer."

Quinn's heart rolled at the admission. She was an orphan, alone in the world. He wanted to wrap her in his arms, tuck her in on his lap and hold her for the rest of the night. Unfortunately they had other things to deal with first. That would have to wait.

"Go back to your conversation with Jamie," Quinn prodded. He was reluctant to cut her off from her memories, but he didn't have a lot of choice in the matter. "What did he tell you when you asked about the check-in photos?"

"Oh, right. I'm sorry. I get scattered sometimes." Rowan ruefully shook her head. "He said that he felt the lines were too long and didn't want to wait in them for a photograph he had no intention of buying. He made some sort of joke about those photographs appealing to women instead of men. That kind of made sense to me so I didn't give it a lot of thought."

"Yeah, I don't think that's out of the ordinary," Quinn agreed. "I think those photos appeal to women and families, but single guys aren't really going to get into the spirit of a cardboard backdrop. Don't you think you would've noticed him in the lobby that day regardless of whether or not he got a photo taken?'"

"Not necessarily," Rowan replied. "I got distracted early because Daphne was complaining about the pink hue in the backdrop. She thought it was the wrong pink – salmon instead of baby pink, as if there's a difference. Then, when I finally took her photo after what felt like hours of complaints, I noticed the omen and called you.

"While I was waiting for you I took photos but was fairly scattered," she continued. "You showed up, we talked, and for the rest of the morning I went through the motions. I didn't go out of my way to notice anything."

"I guess that's fair." Quinn focused on the computer screen, intent. "You said Jamie Dalton, right? That's probably short for James or maybe even Jamison. Let's see what we can find."

Rowan quietly watched Quinn work, marveling at the way he fixated on his screen. The strong bones of his cheeks looked even more pronounced when he adopted his "I'm concentrating" face.

"If you keep looking at me like that I'm going to get distracted," Quinn warned, not glancing up from his screen. "It's giving me ideas."

Rowan giggled. "Ideas?"

"Yes, I'm considering assaulting you with kisses before the night is out."

It was a nice suggestion, but Rowan had a feeling that wasn't going to happen. Still, she didn't want the game to end too quickly. "It's not an assault when I want to help you complete your task. It's a collaboration when that happens."

Quinn smirked. "Duly noted. Okay, here we go."

Curiosity got the better of her and Rowan couldn't

stop herself from shuffling behind Quinn's desk. She had no idea if he felt crowded as she leaned over his shoulder, but she was desperate to see what kind of information he came up with.

"Anything?"

Quinn arched a dubious eyebrow as he cast her a side-long glance. "Seriously?"

"I'm seriously asking," Rowan prodded, refusing to meet his gaze. "If I'm crowding you ... um ... get over it."

Quinn snickered, taking her by surprise when he grabbed her around the waist and tugged her into his lap. She offered up a token fight, but she didn't put a lot of effort behind it because she didn't want to risk an errant elbow taking out Quinn's computer. Once he had her settled Quinn pressed a distracted kiss on her cheek before turning back to the screen.

"You be good while I work," he ordered, tapping on the keyboard.

"I'm working, too."

"You're working on being my lap slave is what you're working on. In fact I ... huh, that's weird."

Rowan turned her head to the screen to see what caught Quinn's attention. "What is it?"

"I can't find anyone with the last name Dalton in our registry. Are you sure that's what he said his last name was?"

"I'm sure. Did you try running various spellings?"

"How many different ways can you spell Dalton?"

"That's a very good point." Rowan tilted her head to the side and tapped her lip. "Sally might know. She's down in the kitchen tonight. I know she was complaining about having to supervise because someone got sick. She was really ticked off, but she had no choice. She's more likely to know the last name. I might've misheard or something."

"And you didn't hear the other guy's name, right?"

Rowan shook her head. "I definitely don't believe I ever heard his full name."

"Well, let's see how many Garys we have," Quinn muttered, typing. The search results only took a few seconds to pop up. "Twenty. We should have photos to go with each registry. Can you look before taking off to track down Sally?"

"Yes." Rowan watched as Quinn skipped from file to file, shaking her head as each photograph filled the screen. When they were done, they'd eliminated every single Gary and still didn't have a match. "That's weird, right?"

"That's extremely weird," Quinn agreed, gently giving Rowan a squeeze before pushing her to a standing position so he could follow suit. He thought better when he paced. "Something bugs me about all of this."

"Other than the obvious, you mean?"

"Obviously."

Rowan smirked at the lame joke. "What are you thinking?"

"I'm thinking that we have a bigger issue than we initially realized," Quinn answered. "I haven't been able to reconcile exactly how Claire Fisher registered on this ship when her fingerprints weren't in the system."

"Oh." Rowan widened her eyes. "I forgot all about that."

"She obviously checked in and bypassed the finger-printing part of the equation, which means someone helped her do it," Quinn said. "Then we have the second set of prints in her room that didn't match anything. Now you add the fact that Jamie and Gary don't happen to be in the system and yet we know they're on the ship and … what does that leave us with?"

"They have an inside man," Rowan finished, awed. "What do you think that means?"

"I have no idea." Quinn frowned when his computer beeped and he leaned forward so he could hit a button, Preston Dickerson's face filling his screen. "That was faster than I anticipated."

"Hello, Mr. Davenport." Dickerson looked shaken. "I've managed to track down some information."

"And?"

"And it's not good."

"Okay, well … hold on a second." Quinn cast an apologetic look at Rowan. "Can you do me a favor and talk to Sally? See what she knows, including if she knows what section of the ship these guys are staying in."

Rowan bobbed her head. "I can do that."

"Whatever you do, don't confront these guys alone," Quinn ordered. "I don't want to tip them off that we're on to them. Find the information and confirm it with the front desk. Make up some reason why you're looking – mismatched photos or something – because if the person helping them is on duty then we're looking at an entirely different level of trouble."

"I've got it." Rowan wanted to kiss him but didn't think it wise considering the computer camera was pointed in his direction. "Will you call me when you have more information?"

"I'll call you the second I'm done with this."

ROWAN FOUND SALLY barking orders in the middle of the main kitchen, her hair pulled back in a severe bun as she glowered at one of her servers.

"Have you completely lost your mind?" Sally

complained. "When someone has a seafood allergy that means they can't have any seafood on their plate."

"Since when is shrimp seafood?" the girl shot back, causing Rowan to bite her lip to keep from laughing.

"Since forever," Sally complained. "That woman had to get an epinephrine shot and now we're going to have to bribe her with freebies to keep her from suing us. Pay more attention next time."

"I still maintain that shrimp isn't seafood."

Sally narrowed her eyes to dangerous slits as she pointed toward the swinging doors that led to the main dining room. "Get out of my kitchen."

Rowan waited until Sally sucked in a steadying breath before launching into her spiel. "I know it's a bad time, but I need your help."

"I don't have time to help you," Sally groused. "I'm never going to catch up as it is. It's so … frustrating. This is why I prefer hiring people to do this part of the job for me." Sally was the head of the entire kitchen staff, but she much preferred creating food masterpieces than delegating authority and ordering people around.

"Well, that doesn't change the fact that I need your help." Rowan launched into a condensed version of what she'd discovered with Quinn, and when she was done, she wasn't surprised to see a shift in Sally's attitude. "So, you see, we need to figure out where these guys are staying."

"Because you think they're killers?"

"Because we think something weird is going on."

"Yeah, well, I've been wondering if something weird was going on with those guys since I found out they were on this ship," Sally muttered, shaking her head. "As for their rooms, I honestly don't know where they're at, but I saw Jamie getting off the elevator on the third floor the other day."

"That helps." Rowan offered a thankful bob of her head. "I don't suppose you know Gary's last name, do you? I couldn't remember it and we can't find a Dalton in the system. It might be because they're both registered under Gary's name."

"He was the quieter of the two," Sally noted, tapping her chin. "I ... Newman. His last name was Newman. I only remember because I got a little drunk that first night and hauled out my *Seinfeld* impressions. They had a Newman character."

Rowan squeezed Sally's arm, relieved. "Thank you. I'm going to run to the lobby and see if whoever is on the desk can track down Gary and Jamie for me. We might actually be getting somewhere for the first time since all of this happened."

"Good luck," Sally said, adopting an angry expression when the waitress she'd been yelling at moments before strolled back into the kitchen. "Now what?"

"Are scallops seafood? They're not, right? They're chicken if I remember correctly."

"I'm so going to fire you the second we dock," Sally barked. "No one can be this stupid without doing it on purpose. You would fall down more if it were something other than an act. I just ... ugh!"

Twenty

"What did you find?"

Quinn was all business when he sat in his chair and squared the computer camera so it was focused on him. He could tell by Dickerson's grave expression that whatever he discovered wasn't good.

"I've been on the phone with the police in Missouri for the better part of the last few hours," Dickerson replied. "Danielle Studebaker is missing. She's been missing for a long time."

"And why was no one alerted? I would think one of the first things they would do is contact the bigwigs at Cara G Cosmetics."

"Because no one realized she was also Daphne DuBois," Dickerson replied. "Apparently Danielle had no idea what she was doing and lucked out when it came to launching the company. She kept all of her paperwork someplace other than her home, because the police didn't stumble across anything that pointed toward Cara G Cosmetics. They seemed surprised when I told them who she was, which means she never even authenticated the Daphne DuBois name."

"I'm not sure what that means."

"Think of it like an author who writes under a pen name," Dickerson suggested. "Even though that person doesn't legally change their name, they have to do a number of things to secure ownership of the moniker. Danielle never did any of that.

"From what I can tell, Danielle was something of a recluse with social anxiety issues," he continued. "She didn't like dealing with people – including accountants, bankers, marketers ... you name it – and she did a really haphazard job when she was putting things together.

"She had no family to report her missing and the house she lived in has fallen into disarray," he continued. "Someone – and I have no idea who, but someone – kept paying the taxes and bills on the house to throw off suspicion."

Quinn rubbed his forehead as he considered the revelation. "So how do the police know Danielle is missing if someone was keeping up the bills?"

"Because six months ago there was a fire and the house burned to the ground," Dickerson answered. "The police started looking into the situation and came up with nothing at every turn. There is no body ... all of the furniture and clothing remained in the house even though it was obvious no one had been inside for years."

"So odds are she's dead." Quinn rolled his neck until it cracked. "What about unclaimed bodies?"

"The cops are searching that right now, but if she was buried in the woods somewhere ... ."

"They may never find her," Quinn finished. "What have you tracked down regarding Claire Fisher?"

"As far as I can tell no one in the company has ever

heard that name." Dickerson looked pained at the admission. "I did some digging myself and found that the Social Security number being used by Claire Fisher belonged to a child who died at birth forty years ago. It looks to me that Claire Fisher stole that child's identity, went through the court system to do a legal name change to Daphne DuBois, and somehow managed to coast from there. The entire thing is mind boggling."

"Don't beat yourself up for it," Quinn offered. "If you weren't looking for something specific it would've been relatively easy for someone with Claire's skill set to pull this off. What do the cops say?"

"I informed them what happened and they're obviously upset because they can't talk to Claire Fisher themselves. From their perspective, they're focused on what happened to Danielle Studebaker. The rest of it really isn't their concern."

"No, it's my concern," Quinn grumbled. "What are the other higher-ups at Cara G Cosmetics saying?"

"They're going into survival mode," Dickerson explained. "They obviously don't want the company to falter but this thing is going to take months to sort out. Danielle Studebaker was the legal owner and she's missing and probably dead. If a body is never found then she has to be declared dead by the courts.

"Now, since she doesn't appear to have any close living relatives, that leaves a bit of a vacuum," he continued. "That means any shirttail relatives she had – cousins, aunts and uncles, any other people who want to put in a claim – are allowed under law to do just that."

"Which probably means that they'll want to sell the company for the money when the dust settles."

"Exactly." Dickerson bobbed his head. "Danielle created the product and then turned it over to a production company to manufacture. The recipe for making the product belongs to her and would be part of the combined intellectual property cache should the company be sold but … it's a big mess."

"So, just so I'm clear, what would happen in the interim?" Quinn asked, legitimately curious. "Say Claire Fisher died and no one knew she wasn't really Daphne DuBois. She must've had a will in place."

"She did and I pulled it." Dickerson shuffled some papers on his desk. "Claire Fisher left everything to her brother, James Fisher, although in the will Daphne DuBois made the bequest to a man she didn't list as family. He was to be the sole proprietor in the event of her death."

Things clicked into place for Quinn, at least partially. "James? I don't suppose you have a photograph of this guy, do you?"

"I ran him." Dickerson shifted a few more folders. "I printed out what I could find. His record isn't much better than Claire's, but he's younger and hasn't done any real time. Ah, here it is." He held up a printed photograph in front of the camera. "I know it's not a great rendering, but that's all I have right now."

Quinn swallowed hard as he studied the photograph. "It's more than enough. I recognize him."

"You do?" Dickerson lowered the photo and arched an eyebrow. "Who is he?"

"He's going by the name Jamie Dalton and he's on this ship right now," Quinn supplied. "He must've killed Claire for the money. I guess that makes sense. She was strangled from behind. A brother wouldn't want to see the life going out of his sister's eyes even if he was a greedy bastard like this guy. What can you tell me about James Fisher? What kind of crimes has he committed?"

"They're all computer crimes," Dickerson supplied.

"He's apparently very good at setting up fake charities and collecting money on crowd-funding websites – he can spin a sob story like you wouldn't believe – and all of his charges stem from that."

"Which also explains how he managed to hide so much information on this ship," Quinn mused. "I'm betting that he somehow hacked our system and changed Claire's fingerprints. They probably worked together to do it. Then something happened between the two of them and he killed her because he knew he would inherit everything."

"I don't have any information on that," Dickerson said. "I can say that, in lieu of the new information, all of Daphne DuBois' accounts and those of Cara G Cosmetics will be frozen. I'm in the process of getting the case in front of a judge and I don't foresee any issues. The only funds allocated will be for payroll."

"That's a good thing," Quinn said. "I don't want James Fisher to have access to a lot of money in case something happens and he manages to run. I should have him in custody before the night is out – as soon as I track him down, of course – and then I'll question him. I'll be in touch with you tomorrow to share what I've found."

"Thank you very much for that." Dickerson looked genuinely relieved. "I will keep pressing the Danielle Studebaker issue. Perhaps we'll get lucky and find an unclaimed body. She should be put to rest. She deserves at least that."

"She deserves more than that but there's only so much we can do," Quinn countered. "I'm going to chase this now from my end. I want to make sure that this guy doesn't have the chance to hurt anyone else. I'll call you tomorrow morning and let you know where things stand."

"I'm looking forward to touching base with you. Good luck."

"Thanks. I'm worried I'm going to need it."

ROWAN WAS FRUSTRATED when she left the main lobby. Despite supplying the clerk behind the front desk with Gary's last name, the girl could find no one to match the description or moniker and Rowan was unable to track down a room.

With nothing better to do – and Quinn busy on his Skype call – she headed to the main deck for a drink at the tiki bar. She figured she could ride out the rest of the evening there, perhaps watch Madison Montgomery herself to make her feel better, and wait for Quinn to arrive and share information.

It seemed like a solid plan, until Rowan ran into Jamie Dalton.

She pulled up short when she caught sight of his familiar features, her heart rolling. She was unsure what to do, opting to buy time by ordering a drink from the bar. Thankfully Demarcus was running things this evening and he gave her a good reason to loiter.

"How are you doing, sweetheart?" Demarcus smirked when she pointed toward the blender. "Piña colada?"

"That's just what the doctor ordered," Rowan replied, mustering a small smile as she hopped up on one of the stools. She risked a glance over her shoulder so she could watch Jamie stare at a group of Cara G Cosmetics representatives before turning back to Demarcus. "How long has he been here?"

"That guy?" Demarcus shrugged. "About an hour or so. Why? Are you already looking to trade Quinn in for a fresher model?"

"Not even remotely." Rowan shook her head as she accepted the drink, fishing out the wedge of pineapple so she could munch on it while spying. "He has a friend. Do you know where he is?"

Demarcus knit his eyebrows together as he glanced between Rowan and Jamie. Her distraction was evident, although he couldn't figure out why she was on deck alone when he saw her sharing an intimate meal with Quinn two hours before. "I haven't seen anyone with him tonight. Are you talking about the blond guy? He was hitting on one of the Cara G Cosmetics women a little bit ago, but I have no idea where he went."

Rowan's heart plummeted. "Which woman? Did you recognize her?"

Demarcus nodded. "It was Penny Parker. I could never forget that name."

"Oh." The admission made Rowan feel better, although only marginally. According to her camera lens, Penny Parker was safe for the time being. That could change but as of now … well … Madison Montgomery was her primary concern. "Has Jamie been hitting on anyone specific?"

"He's been sitting there by himself for the bulk of the night," Demarcus answered, his expression unreadable. "Do you want to tell me what's going on? You're acting weird."

"I'm not sure I'm supposed to tell you," Rowan admitted.

"Try me anyway."

"Well … ." Rowan launched into the sordid tale, keeping it short and sweet as she lowered her voice. When she was done, she focused on Jamie and held her hands palms up. "I don't know what to make of any of it."

"I don't either," Demarcus admitted, moving to the stack of tabs next to the cash register. "I can answer the mystery about the room, though. They've been charging drinks to their room since they arrived."

"Doh!" Rowan slapped her forehead. "That never even occurred to me. I guess that's why I'm not a professional investigator, huh?"

Demarcus shrugged, his lips curving. "You have a professional investigator on your payroll and methinks he probably prefers being paid in kisses, so you lucked out there. I'm sure things even out over the long haul, though. Speaking of Quinn, where is he?"

"He's in his office talking to the Cara G Cosmetics attorney," Rowan replied. "I think the guy found some important information. He looked pretty serious. I figured I would just meet Quinn here when he's done. By the way, I need to text him."

Rowan fished in her pocket until she retrieved her phone, taking a moment to scan a few photos – including one of Penny – to make sure the omen location hadn't changed. Everything remained the same. Madison Montgomery was still in danger and Penny Parker was safe.

"I'm going to text him so he knows where to find me," Rowan said.

"That's a good idea." Demarcus tilted his head to the side as he studied Jamie. "You know, he's acting different tonight than he has during previous visits."

"Does he come here a lot?"

"Every night this week."

"What does he usually do?"

"He picks a woman, hits on her, plies her with drinks, and then disappears with her before it gets too late," Demarcus answered. "Then, the next night, he picks a new woman and does it all over again. I think he's allergic to spending more than one night with the same woman."

"Yeah? Sally said the same thing. In all honesty, I'm not

sure that's unheard of when you're dealing with a guy that age."

"Especially while on a cruise," Demarcus added. "Guys go on cruises strictly to get laid. Still ... now I can't stop watching him given what you said. How do you think he fits into this?"

"I have no idea. We can't be sure he does fit into this. No matter how I run the scenario through my mind, I can't find a reason for him to kill Daphne. It's not as if he knew her."

"Maybe he's working with someone," Demarcus suggested. "Maybe it's the other person who has the motive."

"That's a distinct possibility," Rowan conceded. "As far as we know the only person he's working with is Gary. You haven't seen him talking regularly with anyone else, have you?"

Demarcus shook his head. "I haven't been looking either, though. I see so many faces over the course of a given week that I can't focus on one unless I make a concerted effort. That guy barely ruffled my radar and he's a poor tipper so I saw no reason to focus on him."

"Yeah, I don't know what to think about it," Rowan admitted. "I have trouble believing anyone who doesn't have ties to the company took out Daphne DuBois ... or Claire Fisher, as the case may be. I think it's too coincidental. Plus, well, there's the body fished out of the ocean right before we left. That was a Cara G Cosmetics representative, too."

Demarcus' eyes hopped up his forehead. "Really? I hadn't heard that detail yet. How do you think that plays in?"

"I wish I knew. I don't have an answer. It's a really complicated puzzle."

"Yes, well, I'm sure you'll figure it out." Demarcus patted Rowan's hand as a form of solace. "You're very smart and so is your boyfriend. I don't think anyone can outsmart you, especially a group of saleswomen on a bender because they haven't snagged a vacation in years. Still ... my bet is that you're right. Whoever did this is inside the company. It's probably that assistant. She seems happy since her boss died."

"Yeah, I'm not ruling her out," Rowan agreed. "She has as much reason as anyone to kill Daphne. Plus, now that the truth is out about Claire Fisher, no one in that company is going to see a dime. Whoever killed Claire did it for nothing."

"Oh, really?"

Rowan froze when she heard the voice at her back, stiffening as she swiveled on the stool and locked gazes with Jamie Dalton. Her throat went dry as she swallowed hard, her heart hammering.

"I didn't know you were standing there," Rowan gritted out, her stomach twisting. "I ... um ... ."

"Do you need something?" Demarcus asked pointedly.

"I need answers," Jamie answered, fixating on Rowan. "Sadly, I think you're the only one who will be able to supply them. How about you and I take a walk?"

"Oh, that's a nice offer, but I'm meeting someone." Rowan hated how breathy she sounded. "I think I'll stay here, but you should feel free to enjoy your walk."

Jamie's eyes darkened. "I think not. You're coming with me whether you like it or not."

Twenty-One

"Take your hands off her."

Rowan had never seen Demarcus be anything but friendly and amiable, but his voice was positively dripping with venom when he fixed Jamie with a dark look.

"Listen, bud, this has nothing to do with you," Jamie warned. "I don't want to make a scene or anything ... but mind your own business."

Demarcus remained still for several beats and then bared his teeth, causing Rowan to involuntarily shudder. "If you put your hands on that woman I will break your neck."

Whatever reaction Jamie expected, that wasn't it. "Listen ... ."

"You listen!" Demarcus cut off Jamie with a dark glare. "If you touch her, you're going to be sorry."

Jamie almost looked amused. Almost. Something about Demarcus' expression caused him to take a step back. He held up his hands by way of surrender and made a tsking sound as he swung his chin back and forth. "I just wanted to talk to her, man. There's no reason to get all worked up."

Demarcus didn't stop staring. "Walk away."

"I'm walking."

Demarcus remained rigid until Jamie was a good seven feet away and then he shifted his eyes back to Rowan. She had a wide smile on her face when he slumped his shoulders.

"Oh, that was very impressive," Rowan enthused, quietly clapping her hands in tribute. "If I wasn't already involved with a muscular macho man, I would totally jump you right here and now."

Demarcus' skin was too dark to register blushing, but Rowan could tell he was both pleased and embarrassed. "I didn't do anything."

"Oh, you did something. You're my hero."

"I only stepped in because I figured Quinn would start punching people if something happened to you," Demarcus offered. "I'm strong and tough ... but he works out a lot. I'm pretty sure he could take me."

Rowan snorted. "Stick with me. He's putty in my hands."

"So I've noticed," Demarcus said dryly. "I ... look out!"

Rowan registered the change in Demarcus' demeanor at the last second, smoothly shifting to the side and averting a pair of strong hands as they reached for her shoulders. Rowan was caught off guard and even though she tried to maintain her balance, she toppled to the side and hit the deck on her hands and knees with a loud thud, knocking the wind out of her as pain tore through her left wrist.

"Don't even think about it!" Demarcus roared, moving to launch himself over the counter. He didn't get the chance because that's when Gary swooped in – seemingly out of nowhere – and grabbed the struggling bartender by the throat.

From her vantage point on the ground, Rowan had trouble monitoring exactly what was happening. She could hear Demarcus gasp for breath – and then someone groaned when flesh made contact with flesh – and then things fell eerily silent.

Rowan rolled to her knees as she tried to control her breathing, sucking in gasping mouthfuls of oxygen as she attempted to keep her wits about her. She stared at the deck until Jamie moved in front of her and hunkered down, pressing a finger to the spot beneath her chin and tipping it up.

"I think we need to have a talk."

Rowan openly glared at him. "You're going to be sorry."

"If you open your mouth again, so are you."

"SELENA, HAVE YOU SEEN ROWAN?"

Quinn was confused when he searched the front lobby and found no sign of his missing girlfriend. He stopped by the main kitchen long enough to chat with Sally, getting an earful about stupid people and the definition of seafood before heading toward the lobby. Sally said Rowan was on her way there when she last saw her. By the time Quinn arrived, though, she was gone.

"I have no idea who Rowan is." Selena was young – she'd just turned twenty-one – and Quinn recognized that she harbored something of a crush on him. He tried to ignore her eager smile as he tamped down his frustration.

"Rowan Gray. My girlfriend. She's about yay high with long reddish brown hair, big green eyes and a great smile."

Selena's lips turned down at the corners. "You have a girlfriend? When did that happen?"

"This week. That's hardly the point. Have you seen her?"

"She's the photographer, right?" Selena's mood shifted from bubbly to pouty. "Yeah, I've seen her. She came by asking if we could track down some guy named Gary Newman. She said she accidentally screwed up his photos and needed to find him."

"Did you tell her where to look for this guy?"

"If you ask me, she shouldn't have been hired if she can't keep the photographs straight."

"Selena, I'm not messing around," Quinn warned, tugging on his limited patience. "Did you tell Rowan where to go?"

Selena smirked at the innocent tongue slip. "I can tell her where to go ... if you want me to, I mean."

"Selena!" Quinn's tone was dark and he left no wiggle room when he forced the girl to lock gazes. "Where is Rowan?"

"Oh, um, I couldn't find anyone by the name Gary Newman," Selena supplied, affronted. "We even searched for empty rooms because she thought there might've been a strange error or glitch. We couldn't find anything, though."

"So where did she go?"

Selena shrugged. "I didn't realize it was my turn to babysit her. She's your girlfriend. Why don't you know where she is?"

"Because I was busy with a Skype call," Quinn gritted out.

"So maybe she texted you because she knew you were busy. That's what I would do. Actually, if I were your girlfriend I'd never let you out of my sight. Never. Not even for a second."

"Yes, well, good luck with stalker school," Quinn muttered, digging in his pocket. He frowned when he realized his phone was off. "Crap. I forgot I powered it down when Dickerson called. She probably did leave me a message."

"See, you should've listened to me," Selena sniffed. "I know what I'm talking about. By the way, I wasn't kidding about never letting you out of my sight. I know you made the stalker joke but ... never."

Quinn made an odd face as he took a step away from the woman, focusing on his phone as he waited for the screen to go live. When it did, he exhaled heavily when a text notification popped up in the corner. "She's at the tiki bar waiting for me. Okay."

"Never," Selena repeated, winking as Quinn shuffled toward the door.

"We're probably going to have to revisit those sexual harassment seminars that everyone hated six months ago," Quinn offered. "When I make the announcement I'm going to tell everyone to thank you for their mandatory attendance."

Selena's smile slipped. "You're very mean."

"Yes, but you don't want to stalk me any longer, do you?"

"Oh, no. I still want to stalk you. I'm just going to make sure you don't know when I'm doing it."

"That makes it worse."

Selena shrugged. "I'm not bothered by that in the least."

. . .

ROWAN RUBBED her wrist with her free hand as she sat at the table and stared down Jamie. He was unarmed – as far as she could tell, at least – but his anger was palpable. Her wrist ached, pain coursing through her. Thankfully she could use it as an excuse to remain mildly active while appearing helpless and formulating a plan.

"What are we going to do?" Gary asked from behind the bar, gesturing wildly with the knife Demarcus used to chop fruit. "You blew everything by going after her in front of people. Why couldn't you wait until she was alone?"

"Because she's never alone," Jamie snapped. "We've been trying to get close to her for days and we haven't been able to do it because she's almost always with that security guy. When she's not with him she's with that annoying cook lady. I heard her talking, though, and she knows something."

"What could she possibly know?" Gary argued, his temper getting the better of him. Rowan risked a glance at Demarcus, who sat dazed and confused at the foot of the bar, his eyes unfocused. Gary slammed his head into one of the coolers when he attacked and Rowan couldn't help but worry that Demarcus had a concussion – or possibly something worse. "She's been on this ship with us the entire time. She can't know anything."

"I heard her talking to that guy." Jamie jerked his thumb in Demarcus' direction. "She mentioned Daphne and said something about having to deal with it. Then I heard her say the name Claire Fisher when she thought no one other than the bartender idiot was listening. She clearly knows something."

Gary widened his eyes, surprised. When he turned to Rowan, his face was a mask of decadent evil. "How do you know the name Claire Fisher?"

Rowan knew she didn't have a lot of choices. She could

tell the truth and stall until Quinn showed up or be openly defiant and risk violence. It was an easy choice. "The fingerprints."

"No, I fixed the fingerprints," Jamie snapped. "I hacked the system and wiped Claire's fingerprints. I did it with ours as well." He gestured between Gary and himself. "I've done it before and never had a problem. You're making that up."

"I'm not making it up," Rowan countered, defiant. "You may have wiped the fingerprints in the system, but Quinn collected some as evidence and his search engines are much broader than the ones in the lobby."

"Did you know that?" Gary's tone was accusatory.

"Obviously not," Jamie spat. "What did precious Quinn find?"

Rowan wet her lips, darting her eyes to the table where the Cara G Cosmetics women sat several minutes before. It was empty. They'd either run or been chased out during the melee. Given how drunk they'd been, Rowan had no idea which one was true. "I'm not sure where to start."

Jamie thumped her forehead with the palm of his hand to get her attention. "I would recommend starting at the beginning."

"And don't waste time," Gary added.

"Quinn ran the prints and realized that he had two sets that didn't match our records," Rowan volunteered. "You did well erasing your print records, but you would've done better if you hadn't left prints behind in Daphne's room. On top of that, Daphne's prints matched old criminal records in Minnesota. They weren't hard to match."

"I told her that would be a problem one day," Jamie groused. "Did she listen? No. She never listened. She was such a pain in the ass."

There was something odd about the way Jamie

referred to the dead woman. He knew her well – that much was obvious – but there was another sort of tie hovering right below the surface. It felt almost familial, but Rowan hard no idea how that theory worked.

"Once Quinn realized that Daphne DuBois was really Claire Fisher he started making calls," Rowan supplied, keeping her face neutral as she silently worked through and tried to make sense of Jamie's reaction. "He called the corporate attorney, who admitted that Daphne DuBois was an alias and the real company founder's name was Danielle Studebaker.

"The lawyer and Quinn are trying to find Danielle and figure out why Claire Fisher is impersonating Daphne DuBois," she continued. "Quinn seems to believe there's a very good chance Danielle is dead."

Rowan stared hard at Jamie so she could gauge his reaction. She wasn't disappointed, only it wasn't Jamie who initially reacted.

"Son of a ... I knew we took this too far." Gary swore under his breath as he kicked something behind the bar counter. "I told you that going on cruises and holding conventions was too big of a risk. Did you believe me? Did you listen at all? Of course not. Claire didn't either and look what happened to her."

"Stop talking about Claire," Jamie snapped, his temper flaring. "You know I don't want to talk about her and yet you keep bringing her up. Why?"

Rowan scratched her cheek, the final pieces of the puzzle almost snapping together ... but not quite. She was close to figuring out the ultimate clue and yet she hadn't crossed the finishing line just yet. Thankfully she didn't have to. Someone else picked that moment to join the party – and she served as a monumental distraction for everyone involved.

"What's going on?" Penny asked, glancing around the empty bar. "Did you guys literally chase all of the women away so you have no one else to hit on or something?"

Rowan swiveled in her chair, fixing Penny with a frightened look. "Run. They're dangerous."

Penny stilled, surprised. "Dangerous? I hardly think so."

"They are," Rowan insisted, her tone fervent. "They killed Daphne. They won't hesitate to kill you. You have to run."

Penny didn't look convinced, or perhaps she was merely drunk and couldn't process what Rowan said, but she remained where she was instead of fleeing. "But ... ."

"Run!"

QUINN HELD UP his hands to still the security guards behind him, his eyes dark when they landed on Rowan. When the Cara G Cosmetics women spilled into the main lobby and announced pirates were taking over the ship, he obviously had his doubts. They were drunk and giggling, hardly showing signs of fright. Still, he wanted to be sure so he called for backup. Now he was glad he did.

"The one behind the bar has a knife," he said, keeping his voice low. "I'll be going for him. I need you guys to split up and wait for my signal. You're in charge of grabbing the guy closest to Rowan. He's unarmed and I don't want him putting his hands on her."

The man to Quinn's right nodded. "We'll handle him, sir."

Quinn fervently wished he could be the one to take out Jamie, but since Gary had the knife that wasn't an option. As head of security, he would never ask his men to complete a task he wasn't willing to take on himself. That meant Gary was his responsibility.

"I can see Demarcus over there, too," Quinn whispered. "He looks injured, but I'm too far away to really see what's happening. Have medical on standby because I want him checked out right away."

"Yes, sir."

"Okay, get into your positions," Quinn instructed. "I'm going to try and talk them down first. I don't see that happening, but I have to at least make the attempt. I ... what the hell?" Quinn wrinkled his brow when he saw another figure moving toward the bar. "Crud. There's another civilian involved. It looks like Penny Parker. You're going to have to get her out of harm's way, too."

"We'll handle it, sir."

"Let's do this."

WHY ISN'T SHE RUNNING? Rowan couldn't wrap her mind around the lackadaisical look on Penny Parker's face. Either the woman was drunk or she didn't fully grasp what was happening.

"Penny, you have to get out of here right now," Rowan ordered, her voice taking on a tinge of desperation. "They're crazy ... and dangerous ... and what are you doing?" Rowan's mouth dropped open as Penny hoisted her small body up on one of the barstools. She was calm – calmer than she had any right being – and Rowan had a sneaking suspicion something else was going on.

"I need something to drink, Gary," Penny announced. "Then, once you've done that, you can tell me what's going on. I would love to know why you're holding the ship photographer hostage when we all agreed to lay low until we hit port tomorrow."

Rowan's heart squeezed painfully. "You're involved in this, too, aren't you?"

Penny didn't bother turning around. "Involved? It was my idea. We're going to take over Cara G Cosmetics. Claire did it, after all, so why shouldn't we?"

"But ... who are you people?" Rowan felt sick to her stomach as her gaze bounced between faces. "How did you all get involved with one another?"

"I think I can answer that."

Rowan sucked in a breath when she heard Quinn's voice, swiveling quickly to find him approaching the group from the east. He held his hands up, as if to prove he didn't have a weapon, and he shot her a reassuring smile before focusing on Penny and Gary.

"Oh, well, great," Penny muttered, tugging a hand through her hair as frustration took over. "This just keeps getting worse and worse. I should've seen this coming when I agreed to work with you guys, but I was too greedy to give it the serious thought it deserved."

"I think greed is what cost all of you," Quinn interjected, casting a warning look at Jamie when the man shuffled closer to Rowan. "If you touch her I will rip your heart out of your chest and feed it to you."

Unlike when Demarcus issued his threat, Jamie had the good sense to take Quinn at his word. He visibly gulped, paled a bit, and then took a step away from Rowan. "I don't want to hurt her. If you force my hand, though, you're not going to like the outcome."

"If your hand goes anywhere near her, you're not going to like the sound of breaking bones that will accompany your death," Quinn spat. "Don't even look at her."

"Fine." Jamie rolled his eyes as he took another step away from Rowan.

"Oh, bravo," Penny intoned, making a face. "That was

downright heroic. You're a man after my own heart. Are you sure you want to stick with her? I'm about to become a very wealthy woman and I'm sure I could find a place for you in my operation."

"You're not about to become anything," Quinn countered. "Preston Dickerson, the corporate attorney for Cara G Cosmetics, in case you've never heard that name, is having the accounts frozen even as we speak. As for the port you mentioned, that's not happening either. The captain put the kibosh on the stop earlier in the day, and once I realized what was happening here, I sent a full security detail to his office. He's untouchable, and much like the U.S. government, we don't negotiate with terrorists on the Bounding Storm."

Penny's mouth dropped open. "You're making that up."

"I'm not," Quinn shot back. "We knew something was amiss when we realized that Daphne DuBois was really a wanted grifter from Minnesota. Dickerson is trying to track down Danielle Studebaker right now. We know she's dead, but he's moving for all of Cara G Cosmetics' financials to be frozen until things can be sorted out.

"That means, James Fisher, that you won't inherit a thing because your sister didn't really own the company," he continued, his eyes flashing when they locked with Jamie's. "You're not getting one thing."

"I knew it!" Penny hissed, smacking her hand against the bar. "I knew this would go south. Why couldn't you just listen to me when I told you to wait, Jamie? No. You couldn't do it. You had to come on this ship even though I told you it was a bad idea. Then you got in a fight with your sister and now look where we're at!"

"I figured it had to be you, Jamie," Quinn said, bobbing his head. "You couldn't look her in the eye when you were doing it, could you? That's why you attacked from behind. She was drunk, but she recognized you and let you into her room. You thought you had everything covered when you hacked the registry – that was smart, by the way, and I can't wait to hear how you accomplished it – but you didn't count on me using outside search engines to run the prints in the room."

"I guess I'm better with computers than security procedure," Jamie sneered.

"It really doesn't matter," Quinn said. "I'm just curious how you three got together. How long ago did you start planning your takeover? Oh, wait, let me guess. Claire was a mean and nasty boss and Penny accidentally bonded with Jamie at some point and the truth came spilling out. Am I close?"

"Pretty close," Penny conceded. "Jamie and I were involved for a bit. We didn't last because of his roving eye, but I didn't forget what he told me about Claire. I realized I had a great chance to take over the company if I played my cards right. Unfortunately for me, I partnered with idiots and now I'm stuck with nothing."

"You're stuck with worse than nothing because you're going to prison," Quinn supplied. "You were better off before you killed Claire. Why didn't you simply blackmail her?"

"I tried, but it didn't work," Penny muttered. "When Jamie and Gary first showed up I knew they wanted to kill her right away. In fact they were going to do it on the beach but had to settle for some other poor sap who heard us planning how we were going to steal the company. I told them it was a bad idea, but they didn't listen. It took me forever to talk them out of it and I promised to blackmail Claire myself if they would just hold off. When I did, though, she laughed at me."

"That's because Claire knew what you didn't," Quinn supplied. "She knew that you couldn't blackmail her without taking down the entire company. So, yeah, you might've had a certain amount of power, but Claire knew as well as anyone that if you used that power no one would get anything."

"I didn't mean to kill her like I did," Jamie offered, morose. "She was out of control that night, though. She kept yelling that I was stupid. She was upset because you wouldn't pay her the attention she thought she deserved. I just … snapped."

"I don't understand," Gary pressed. "Does this mean we're not going to get rich?"

"It means we're not going to get anything." Penny drained her drink and got to her feet. "Give me the knife, Gary."

Gary balked. "This is our only weapon."

"And are you really going to try and use it?"

"There's only one guy," Gary said, lowering his voice to a conspiratorial whisper. "I can take one guy."

"No, you can't," Quinn countered. "You have no chance of taking me."

"Besides that, there's more than one guy." Penny jerked her chin in the direction of the shadowed deck over her shoulder. "He's got men surrounding us. I've seen them moving in the dark and we're outnumbered … by a long shot. We have no chance of escape. I guess, in theory, we could jump over the side of the ship. I'm guessing, however, that sort of death is going to be worse than going to jail."

Rowan kept her hands flat on the table as she watched Quinn work. She was fascinated by his technique, and the raw resignation Penny displayed as she prepared to surrender. "Do you wish you didn't do it?" The question was out of Rowan's mouth before she thought better of uttering it. "Do you wish you would've done something else?"

Penny flicked her eyes to Rowan and shrugged, briefly wrapping her fingers around the knife handle as Gary dropped it in the palm of her hand. "I wish a lot of things. Mostly I wish I didn't let myself become this ... person ... I see in the mirror every morning. I saw Claire go the easy route and prosper. I thought that I could do it, too."

Penny heaved out a sigh before resting the knife on the counter and taking a step back. "There are no easy routes in life. I knew that and yet somehow I forgot it."

"Yeah? Well, you're going to have plenty of time to think about it in prison," Quinn said, gesturing for Gary to walk out from behind the bar. "Now, if everyone will remain still, I promise we'll process you as quickly as possible."

Rowan watched him work for the next few minutes, only getting up to check on Demarcus and wait with him while the medical team checked him over. Once Jamie, Gary, and Penny were in custody, Quinn hurried to Rowan and Demarcus so he could look them over with his own eyes.

"Are you okay?" Quinn tugged Rowan to him, smoothing her hair. "He didn't hurt you, did he?"

"I hurt myself a bit when I fell off the stool, but otherwise I'm fine."

"Good." Quinn kissed her forehead and focused on Demarcus. "What about you?"

Demarcus' eyes were glassy. "I hit my head."

"I heard. We're going to take you to medical for observation tonight. Is that okay?"

Demarcus shrugged. "I hit my head."

"Yeah, you're a little out of it." Quinn kept his arm around Rowan's waist as he shuffled to the side to make room. "We're docking early tomorrow. We're on course to hit the mainland before eight. We'll handle the bulk of this then."

Demarcus offered a half-hearted wave. "Cool. Did I mention I hit my head?"

Quinn chuckled. "It's hard. You'll survive."

Twenty-Two

"I was starting to worry you forgot about me."

Rowan glanced up from the water where she waded and fixed Quinn with a worried smile as he heaved out a sigh and sank to the sand. They were on the mainland for the day, the prisoner transfer taking place in the early morning hours while the bulk of the Bounding Storm's staff dealt with disgruntled guests. Despite the murder and potential trouble the night before, the guests didn't want to cut short their vacations. Rowan was thrilled that she didn't have to deal with the complaints.

Despite his obvious weariness, Quinn returned the smile and gestured for her to come closer. "I could never forget about you. Come here."

Rowan automatically did as he instructed, although she couldn't tamp down the building worry in the pit of her stomach. "Is everything okay?"

"Yes." Quinn patted his lap. "Hop on."

Rowan arched an eyebrow, surprised. "You want me to sit on your lap? It's ninety degrees out here."

"And you're in a little dress, there's a breeze, and I

really want to touch you."

Rowan's smile was gentler this time and she slid between his knees so she could nestle her back against his chest. "Better?"

"I'm tired, but this is definitely better." Quinn pressed a kiss to her cheek as he ran his hands over her shoulders. "It's done. The local police have taken all three of them into custody."

"I figured as much when I read your text."

"I'm sorry about that." Quinn's expression was rueful. "I wanted to call you, but I was running low on time."

"I would like to think I'm not so needy that I don't understand it when you have to deal with murderers. I'm okay." Rowan patted his hand. "I'm fine. In fact, I shared a nice and leisurely breakfast with Sally while you were up before the sun. I'm probably better off than you right now."

"I'm okay." Quinn said the words, but his sigh told another story. "Do you want to hear it?"

"Part of me doesn't, but it will drive me crazy if I don't."

"Danielle Studebaker is dead. Claire and Jamie poisoned her dinner five years ago. They befriended her, lied to her, learned as much as they could about the company, gained access to the bank accounts, and then they killed her. Claire proceeded to take over the Daphne DuBois persona and it happened pretty much how I theorized. She slowly replaced workers and started raking in the dough.

"At first Jamie and Claire were happy with their haul," he continued. "They couldn't believe that they managed to fool everyone and skimmed a ton of money from the company. At a certain point they realized they could run a long con and perhaps never get caught.

"Gary and Jamie were friends in high school and they brought him on later," he said. "He did various tasks without being a familiar face at the company in case they needed to use him for something else. Jamie handled most of the computer work, but Gary did a lot of the heavy lifting. When Jamie and Penny got involved, he let Claire's real identity slip when he was drunk one night. That's when the greed went into overdrive.

"It seems that Claire wanted to keep the bulk of the money for herself since she was taking on all of the risk and Jamie and Gary thought it should be an even split," Quinn explained. "That caused a riff … blah, blah, blah … and Penny, Jamie and Gary decided to blackmail Claire into giving them what they wanted."

"We both know that didn't work," Rowan noted. "Had they really thought it through they would've realized that. I guess greed overrules rationality, huh?"

"Yeah. Jamie approached Claire when she was drunk and wanted her to sign a contract giving him half the company. She called him names and treated him terribly so he snapped and killed her."

"Do you think he would've killed her under different circumstances?"

"I can't answer that," Quinn replied. "I think perhaps Claire was always destined for death. She helped create the situation and, not that she deserved to die, she did kill another woman so I can't muster a lot of sympathy for her."

"What about Danielle's body?"

"Jamie is going to take police to the location as part of his plea bargain. He's also going to go into great detail about how he managed to hack our computer system. We're looking at some massive upgrades there."

"They're going to give him a deal?" Rowan couldn't

help but be surprised. "Why?"

"Because this is a mess and they don't want it to wind through the court system for years," Quinn answered. "It's pretty straightforward now. They'll all do at least forty years for Danielle's death – which Gary wasn't around for but knew about after the fact – and Claire's murder. That's on top of the sales representative who overheard them plotting before we left port. They admitted to killing her, too. Aside from that, Cara G Cosmetics will probably survive in some form, although I have no idea what."

"Well, I'm not sure if that's a good or bad thing, but I'm glad all of those women won't be losing their livelihood."

"You and me both."

The duo lapsed into comfortable silence as Quinn pressed his eyes shut and enjoyed the feeling of Rowan's body pressed against his. After a few minutes of quiet contemplation, Rowan broke the silence first.

"I figured out the hopping death omen, if that matters to you, by the way."

Quinn stirred, surprised. "You did? How?"

"Penny said that Jamie and Gary wanted to kill Claire right away when they arrived on the ship," Rowan volunteered. "That's how she earned the death omen that day. Penny talked them out of it and then blackmailed Claire, who I think was planning on killing Penny to keep her secret safe.

"You know that night she claimed someone attacked her? I'm pretty sure she made it up," she continued. "She was laying the groundwork for something to happen to Penny. She wanted us to believe the sales representatives were at risk."

"I guess that makes sense," Quinn mused. "What about Madison Montgomery?"

"I'm not sure on that one," Rowan conceded. "Perhaps she was due to find out the secret, too. Maybe she already knows, for that matter. Maybe she was going to join in on the blackmail. I'm not sure it matters. She's safe now."

"She is," Quinn agreed, pulling Rowan's hair behind her shoulder so he could kiss the tender spot behind her ear. "I'm happy to put this one behind us."

"Me, too. Now we can focus on us."

"Yup."

"Does that mean you want to have sex?"

Quinn was taken aback by the blunt nature of the question. "Right now? I think I'd like to wait until we have a bit of privacy. I would rather not be arrested for indecency."

Rowan chuckled, genuinely amused. "Not right now. Sally asked me over breakfast if we celebrated last night's death-defying antics with sex. She's very disappointed in us."

"Well, as big of a fan as I am of … um … sex, I would prefer waiting a bit," Quinn admitted. "I would rather get to know you better before worrying about that. There's no need to rush."

"Really?" Rowan couldn't hide the relief from her voice. "You don't mind that everyone will be watching us?"

Quinn pursed his lips as he shook his head. "I don't mind at all. In fact, I insist on it. I'm happy learning everything there is to know about you and getting to that point when we're both ready. I'm not living my life on someone else's schedule."

"I agree."

"I figured you would." Quinn brushed his lips over her ear. "That doesn't mean I'm not interested in you assaulting me with kisses whenever the mood strikes."

"That goes double for me."

"Good." Quinn and Rowan exchanged a sweet kiss before Quinn shifted to get a bit more comfortable. "Okay, where did we leave off?"

"What's your favorite television show?" Rowan asked, not missing a beat.

"Old or new?"

"Does it matter?"

"Absolutely."

"Old."

"*MacGyver*. I always loved that show. I thought I could make a bomb out of a gum wrapper when I was six and was terribly upset when nothing happened."

Rowan snickered, amused. "This is kind of nice, right?"

"It's very nice. Your turn. What's your favorite old television show?"

"*Little House on the Prairie*."

"Seriously?"

"Yup."

"Huh. You're a complicated woman."

"That's probably not going to change," Rowan pointed out. "The death omens aren't going anywhere."

"I don't care about that," Quinn said, and he honestly meant it. "I happen to like my women complicated."

"And addicted to crab legs."

"That, too." Quinn heaved out a sigh. "What's your favorite new television show?"

Rowan giggled as she shifted on his lap. "Do you think this will ever get old?"

"Nope. For some reason I think this will always feel new."

Rowan didn't know why, but she agreed with him. She couldn't wait to find out, though. For them, the adventure had just begun.

Made in the USA
Monee, IL
31 May 2022

97309344R00135